Hard to Swallow – Easy to Digest

By Mark Wheeller
Scheme of Work by Karen Latto

Additional contributions by Adrian New, Fiona Spargo-Mabbs, Sarah Blackman various members of the original Oaklands Youth Theatre development team and cast 1988-1990

Design and Layout by Karen Latto

Pping Publishing
Southampton UK

Wheellerplays.com

© Mark Wheeller / Karen Latto 2017
ISBN: 978-0-9575659-3-7

Cover photograph by Bill Giles
Cover design by Charlotte Askew

Published by Pping Publishing, Southampton, UK.
First Edition 2017

www.wheellerplays.com

www.karenlatto.com

Enquiries should be made to Wheellerplays@gmail.com

Hard to Swallow – Easy To Digest

A CIP catalogue record for this book is available from the British Library

Printed by Book Printing UK
Remus House, Coltsfoot Drive, Peterborough, PE2 9BF

Acknowledgements

All the sources for kind permission to use their word in both this book and the original play: "Ann", Donna McInnally Batt, Sarah Blackman, Richard Brown, Christine Farleigh, Josh Jordan, "Martha", Adrian New, Debra O'Sullivan, Fiona Spargo Mabbs, Wade Williams and Chris Vaudin.

Maureen Dunbar (in particular her book Catherine published by Penguin books), John, Richard, Simon, Catherine (diaries) and Anna Dunbar. Dr Tony Saunders and Just Seventeen.

The writing team and performers in the original play: Donna Batt, Martin Blackman, Sarah Blackman, Richard Brown, Paula Curtis, Jason Eames, Debra Giles, Deanne McAteer, Kate Noss, Abigail Penny, Gary Richards, Kalwant Singh, Sharon Tanner and Chris Vaudin.

Roy Nevitt and the wonderful Drama department at Stantonbury Campus Theatre for introducing me to Documentary Theatre.

Peter Hollis, Pete Vance and Joan Winter and all those in charge at Oaklands for making Drama a high priority in their School.

Adrian New and Steven Pearce from StopWatch Theatre Company.

Fiona Spargo Mabbs for writing about her conversation with Maureen.

Meg Davis & Sophie Gorell Barnes and MBA Literary Agency for continued belief.

Rachael Wheeller: The great woman behind the barely adequate man.

Peter Rowlands from Act Now Plays (CUP) for first publishing an early version of the play.

Dawn Boyfield, Evie Efthimiou and Lynda Taylor from dbda now Zinc Publishing for their belief in all things Wheellerplays.

Barrie Sapsford for his support and inspiration from *The Story Behind Too Much Punch For Judy*.

Charlotte Askew for her continued support and cover design.

Ali Clarke from Romsey School for taking on the production which led to my setting up RSCoYT and presenting the little goat scenes.

Bill Giles - Debra's dad, for his superb photographs taken throughout the two years we were working on Hard to Swallow. He stayed on to be the OYT official photographer for years after Debra had left. All his time working with us was entirely voluntary.

Bob Singleton and the Drama Department and students at Houston School For Performing and Visual Arts for their amazing welcome to our team. Jackie and Leo Rundstein for their generosity and hospitality Rachael Ollie and myself during our stay in Houston.

Photographs/Images

Cover: Bill Giles
Pages 1 & 56: From Sarah Blackman's personal collection.
Pages 8, 17, 19, 24, 33, 40, 44, 51, 52, 53, 75, 76, 83, 86, 89, 90: From Mark Wheeller's collection
Pages 10 & 91: Southern Evening Echo – from Mark Wheeller's scrapbook.
Page 12: Ape Theatre Company
Page 19: Maureen Dunbar's personal collection.
Pages 23, 36, 38, 42, 64, 69, 71. 74, 75, 81, 88. Bill Giles
Page 27: Sunday Times Colour Supplement
Pages 43 & 51: John Rowley's original poster design.
Page 57: Posters by Chris Vaudin and Paul Harris.
Page 132: Fiona Spargo-Mabbs/Maureen Dunbar's personal collections.
Page 139: Chris Webb
Page 144: Ascott Photos

Hard to Swallow Timeline

May 13th 1987	Mark Wheeller appointed to Oaklands Community School, Southampton and to found the Oaklands Youth Theatre (OYT)
May 26th 1987	Maureen grants Mark Wheeller permission to adapt her book Catherine for the Epping Youth Theatre to present. (The plan to start would be delayed as Mark has a new job and needs to establish his new Youth Theatre group in Southampton – Oaklands Youth Theatre aka OYT).
February 1st 1988	The proposed OYT cast for Catherine meet Maureen at Oaklands.
July 7/8th 1988	First performance of Catherine at Oaklands Community School, billed as a preview so that our official premiere could happen at the Fringe.
July 14th 1988	Fareham Arts Centre
August 29th – September 3rd 1988	Edinburgh Festival (Fringe) Official Premiere (Heriot Watt Theatre).
January 12th 1989	London University Institute of Education (Invited schools)
January 27/28th 1989	Oaklands Community School (adjudication by NT)
March 14th 1989	Sholing Girls School Southampton
April 6th 1989	Totton Drama Festival (Winning Best Youth Production)
April 30th 1989	Malvern Girls College
July 7/8th 1989	Oaklands Community School
July 12th 1989	The Royal National Theatre as part of the Lloyds Bank National Theatre Challenge.
July 1990	Oaklands Community School
September 1990	16 performances of both Hard to Swallow or Too Much Punch For Judy in a range of schools, universities and medical institutions across 3 weeks in Houston Texas.
October 1990- December 1990	Stopwatch Theatre Company perform Hard to Swallow in 25 schools from Bristol to Blackpool!
1991	Published by Cambridge University Press – Act Now Series
2000	Published by dbda (now Zinc Publishing)
2005	Published by Maverick Plays in Australasia (until 2015)
2015	Published by Zinc Publishing as an iBook
2016	Became a set text for the Eduqas GCSE Drama 9-1
2017	Romsey School film the play for the official Wheellerplays DVD along with RSCoYT's first ever performance of "Crossing the Bridge – The Unseen Billy Goat Plays"

Contents

Chapter 1

OYT – An Extraordinary New Youth Theatre

THEATRE REVIEW

By Ann McFerran – The Stage and Television Today

Oaklands Youth Theatre was one of 12 groups chosen by the National Theatre from hundreds of entries throughout the UK to play at its three-day festival, sponsored by Lloyds Bank. Devised with the help of its director, the veteran youth theatre worker Mark Wheeller, this highly talented company has developed a drama on anorexia, focussing on the tragic story of Catherine Dunbar. Elegantly structured, highly informative and imaginatively theatrical, the piece is a model of the kind of devised theatre which manifests the young people's involvement throughout the working process.

This review, in the prestigious Stage Newspaper, was more complimentary than we could possibly have hoped for but what really tickled me and stuck in my memory, was the term 'veteran' being applied to me... I was only 31! Nevertheless, I took it as a compliment. It suggested some additional weight to what I considered to be my slender achievements.

I had been working as a Youth Theatre director for just 10 years. Oaklands, was my third company. Stantonbury, the first, in Milton Keynes (1979-82), Epping, the second (1982-87) and then Oaklands (1987- 2017). It was 1989 and *Hard to Swallow* was my first original production with OYT. We had been nearly two years making it!

My only notable credits up until this point in time were:

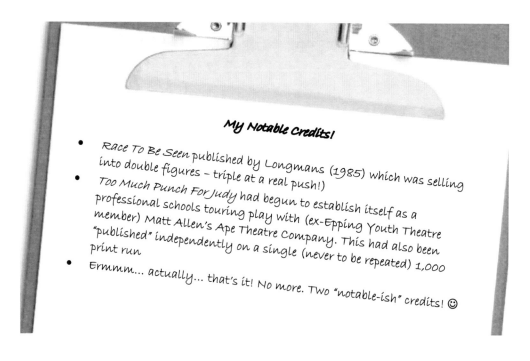

My Notable Credits!

- *Race To Be Seen* published by Longmans (1985) which was selling into double figures – triple at a real push!)
- *Too Much Punch For Judy* had begun to establish itself as a professional schools touring play with (ex-Epping Youth Theatre member) Matt Allen's Ape Theatre Company. This had also been "published" independently on a single (never to be repeated) 1,000 print run
- Ermmm... actually... that's it! No more. Two "notable-ish" credits! ☺

The cast who performed at the National Theatre that day were 'ordinary kids' from a new Community Comprehensive School, placed on an estate to bring 'hope' to the area. To me, these young people were anything but ordinary. My expectations were that they should be extraordinary... and they were! They worked 3 hour rehearsals, two nights a week, for two years to create this "imaginatively theatrical" piece of work. I look back and wonder why they made such an incredible commitment. There's no better way to find out than to ask them...

> *I never thought of it as a commitment. It was something I relished. Youth Theatre was something different and became a second family for me. At 15, I was going through a parental break up, hard for most, but OYT kept me going. It was my escape. Pressure to deliver scenes and then performance was a worthwhile goal. I will never forget the camaraderie.*

Richard Brown (then aged 14-16 and played Simon, Catherine's brother)

This camaraderie was crucial for success. My motto has always been:

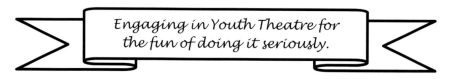

Engaging in Youth Theatre for the fun of doing it seriously.

As a group, we had a sufficiently strong (and real) bond, and we could experiment with ideas knowing not all of them will work. Failure could not be eliminated, but the fear of failure would be. These real bonds (and I mean real) paid off in other ways for them… and of course for me!

Teacher or Youth Group leader?

A crucial aspect of this was the use of first name terms between all of us (me included)[1]. This symbolised an equality. Our relationships would never be equal (none are), but I was keen to remove any idea of deference and did this across all who I taught as well as the Youth Theatre group. It is a key feature in any success I have had. I was a new teacher in a new school. This group of young people put their trust in me and their support helped me in the various classes they were in. The positive relationship I had with them was a huge benefit to me, and with potentially more difficult students who were their friends.

A key reason for having a Youth Theatre as part of my department, was for the YT members to cascade their advanced devising skills into the school drama curriculum. This served to raise standards in Drama across the whole school. OYT's performances offered a model of how such work should be done.

At this time, the Drama GCSE exams heavily weighted students' ability in devised work. In my first year at Oaklands, improvements showed in the school Drama exam results. Examiners often said we had a "house style". Some incredibly brave and exciting work was produced in this era. Success snowballed. I have never understood Drama teachers who don't choose to use the School Production to add value to their curriculum drama. All too often these are two parallel activities. For me, curriculum and extra-curriculum were totally integrated. It was, I think, a win/win for all of us…

I loved it! Simple as that. I have precious memories of OYT. The creative process, working as a group with friends and those running OYT was one of the most formative parts of my secondary education and teenage years. To have the opportunity and space (literal & creative) to develop ideas and to perform – was huge.
I grew up in a very happy but 'normal' working class family – so, to have this level of investment in 'me' and what potential I could achieve, was profound. I absolutely loved it. I once described my OYT experiences as a fairy-tale and Mark, my fairy Godmother. Drama and acting as an aspiration will always be my, 'what if?' Young, tender dreams need to be managed so carefully. Actually, I've been very lucky and have had fantastic jobs/experiences in my life but, making the steps from being in a safe space and exploring so creatively, then going out into the real world and being able to carry it through is hard. It can feel like an indulgence.

Debra Giles (then 13-14 and was part of the ensemble before playing Maureen)

---

[1] I had previously taught at Stantonbury Campus in Milton Keynes, where all staff across the school were addressed by their first names. It left an indelible mark on me. I am proud to say I remained "Mark" throughout my teaching career and was only challenged about it once when Oaklands was Academised. After a protracted debate, it was agreed I would continue as "Mark".

Throughout my five years in Epping (1982-87) I had sunk myself into work committing myself to it day and night. I was perhaps a workaholic. In Southampton things were changing. I had to try and balance a new girlfriend and a personal life as well… or perhaps more accurately, she had to learn to live with my commitment to OYT. I had met Rachael on my first day at Oaklands and would, while we were developing *Hard to Swallow*, marry her with all the Youth Theatre members at our wedding!

I remember, to my shame, saying to her:

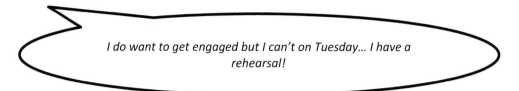

I do want to get engaged but I can't on Tuesday… I have a rehearsal!

Not the most romantic proposal… but it was the way things were. Rehearsals were central to my life.[2]

That said, we were really 'just another Youth Theatre'. In fact, not even that. As a new teacher, very few of the older students were prepared to buy into the different ways of this new, younger and less experienced Drama teacher. Only two over 16's joined. It was a very young, fifteen-strong group, made up of predominantly 13-15 year olds.

I invited them to be involved as I felt they had shown promise after I directed a revival of my *Race to be Seen*. This production served as a model of what was possible with an original documentary style production. It also, unbeknown to them, served as a very long and detailed audition for what was to become *Hard to Swallow*.

No one had any idea then that we would create a play that would be read and studied in schools across the world. We would have laughed at the thought! All we wanted was to develop the best production we could. I wanted to generate, wanted to survive in my job. I had to keep the participants engaged, not easy with such a long preparation period.

I stress; none of us had a star-studded background. None had appeared on the professional stage, nor on TV (to my knowledge). None knew anyone who had had any success in the Performing Arts. We were a brand-new Youth Theatre group wanting to put ourselves on the map, initially aiming to make an impression in our local community… and perhaps, I hoped, beyond!

Sarah Blackman, then 16-18, told me about her previous experience, something at the time I knew little about. When I first asked Sarah to write something for me I anticipated a few pages. As you will see, Sarah has written her own book within a book and it adds so much detail and colour to what I have sat down to convey!

---

[2] Rachael read this and said: With hindsight you were convinced that your total immersion in OYT was completely justified and a given. I just had to put up with it being your "normal". I was happy to do so. I knew it was worthwhile and very special."

I'd been creating public performances and re-enactments of favourite stories before I knew what 'theatre' or 'drama' meant. For me this was 'playing,' alongside bike riding and climbing trees. I'd post invitations through neighbours' letter boxes asking them to watch a performance of 'Rumpelstiltskin' for example. Assuming they'd need an incentive, I included a raffle ticket… a chance to win a coveted prize such as that week's Beano or a pencil sharpener! Possibly the most amusing part about this is that people did turn up and watch!

I happily volunteered for every solo, sketch or audition at Junior and Middle school. I was always a strong (loud and confident!) singer and, even at nine, was determined to play featured parts. I never questioned my motivation or interest in performing. I did question why other people didn't share my interest, why they couldn't sing in tune, or embody different characters, vary their voices or adopt accents!

I remember being hugged by the city mayor, after playing the Artful Dodger in 'Oliver!' who couldn't understand how a 10-year-old from Hampshire could sound like an urchin from Bermondsey. In contrast, the boy who played Oliver, had no real aptitude or interest. He had to be pushed on stage when it was his cue, whereas I'd still be telling him to 'consider himself at 'ome' right now if I could! By the time I was 12, I'd joined two independent theatre groups. One was for children. It soon became clear, I had different expectations from the others. They wanted to spend most of the session on "games". I wanted to move on to the 'real' stuff; creating scenes, and a challenge, put to the test by the very first scenario we were given; 'being attacked by marauding Triffids'.

The second was an amateur dramatic company for adults. Here I was lumped into the 'chorus' to be shunted on and off stage when we were needed to cover holes in the backcloth! The adults, with varying degrees of success, battled with their scripts, and often asked mid-scene "Are we going to the Rising Sun or the White Horse afterwards?"

I felt under-used and disconnected to the material which felt cold, rigid and adult-centric. It marginalised any intellectual or creative input from somebody of my age. The opportunity to create something new never materialised in these settings. Rehearsals were entrance and exit orientated and there was never any impetus to explore a character's emotional-self, beyond a stereotype or caricature. Everything felt one-dimensional.

Unbeknown to me at that time, I would soon find a door opening, encouraging me to take full responsibility for every aspect of building a performance.

Sarah Blackman (Ensemble in the original production)

By this point, I had built up fairly significant experience of curating documentary/verbatim plays. This was, I was to find, an important difference. I was well on my way to being a 'veteran' in this respect! I still wanted the process to be equal but began to realise that it wasn't.

Not knowing any other way of working, I worked with them as though they had the same experience as me and included them in every decision, every step of the way. But sometimes I felt I needed to make unilateral decisions to speed things up. I did more work on the script at home (much as I had done with *Too Much Punch for Judy*[3]) which made this process the final one where I included the cast in developing the actual script as opposed to the staging of the piece. My current Youth Theatre groups still retain a strong guiding hand on how my productions are staged but have far less input to the script. They do have something to offer but now take on a role of checking my (lack of) cultural modernity.

I'd been involved in school drama, playing 'bit' parts and extra-curricular dance/musical theatre groups where my initial passion for performance started. 'Hard to Swallow' was a different level of engagement. We devised the piece as a group based on research, family interviews and input from Catherine's mother, and participated in workshops with Mark and visiting professionals. It was totally immersive. Looking back, I appreciate even more what a huge responsibility we had taken on – not only to develop, explore and present the ideas and subject matter carefully, but to Catherine's family.

Debra Giles, (Ensemble in the original production)

The start of Hard to Swallow

In this production, the cast had the advantage of having me structuring, editing and enhancing the play throughout the preparation period. I had the advantage of their fresh eyes and ideas as, increasingly, they developed a new, uninhibited theatrical vocabulary. I expected a lot from them… and most of the time they delivered! Their input enlivened the often-dense paragraphs of writing which inadvertently forced an imaginative approach to the staging.

I think we all underappreciated the trust Maureen put in us. She didn't know or know of me at all. I spoke to Maureen this year and her memory was that she asked to meet us before offering us

---

[3] *The Story Behind Too Much Punch for Judy* by Mark Wheeller (Pping) tells this story.

permission. The truth is quite different. I wrote to her asking permission in early May 1987, before I was appointed to Oaklands Community School. Her response on 26th of May 1987 (by which time I had been appointed) said the following... and she was obviously under the impression that I would be developing this play with my (more) established Epping Youth Theatre group.

Dear Mark,

Thank you for your letter and for your comments about my book "Catherine".

I am very touched that you should want to use Catherine's life as a basis for a documentary play. You have my full permission to do so. There is however a film being made by ITV based on the book which will be shown on all networks either at the end of June or July. You would have to gain clearance from them should you still wish to go ahead. If you like, I will speak to the person concerned and let you know his reply.

Anything that can be done to highlight the danger and the anguish of anorexia is very worthwhile.

Should you decide (and are able) to go ahead with the play I will be happy to help you with any background information you may need.

Very best wishes to you all at the Epping Youth Theatre,

Maureen Dunbar.

It is incredible that Maureen gave me her permission, especially given that a prime-time TV film had also been made. Maureen didn't meet me or the cast until the group who would put the play on was in place.

We met Maureen on the 1st February 1988. She talked openly but some of the cast found her 'distant'. I wondered at the time whether that would change. Looking back, I imagine they were overawed. I described her in my diary (which, sadly I gave up writing just before the performances) as 'nice'. I also wrote:

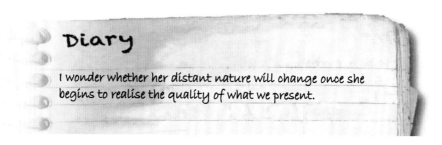

Diary

I wonder whether her distant nature will change once she begins to realise the quality of what we present.

I certainly didn't lack confidence!

The whole development team were given the time off school because it was deemed an important meeting. The local newspaper came along to report on the event (pictured below).

For Maureen, I see this as an incredible example of blind trust. At the time, surprisingly, I didn't think about it in any depth... and neither, it seems, did the YT members.

As an enthusiastic teen who believed very strongly in the medium of theatre to make an impact on people's lives, it made perfect sense to me that Maureen Dunbar would allow us, an unknown entity with no track history of working together from a different socio-economic background, to be responsible for publicly portraying her story. I took her trust in our abilities for granted.

As an adult, I cannot believe she agreed! I am blown away by her braveness to do so and the risk she took. I remember her saying her belief was that people close to Catherine's age when she began to suffer from anorexia would have more of a simpatico relationship with her daughter.

Maureen bestowed upon us:
- private documents
- memoirs and hitherto unshared information
- leads to people close to Catherine who had played an important part in her life
- cassette tapes of music that Catherine had listened to
- access to her daughter's psychological mind-set via Catherine's personal diaries.

Of all the information given to us for research purposes, Catherine's diaries, felt almost sacrosanct to me, verging on intrusion.

I remember devouring them in one sitting, desperately trying to connect with this young woman. I was searching for clues to whatever issues in her life had led her to this "peculiar action" of strict management, and denial of food. Was her anorexia a psychological cause or a symptom?

We were undoubtedly affected by the material. I might even suggest that we needed to be, in order to honour it. But, come curtain down, we had the choice of how much we 'took with us' back into our real life. It is a most humbling realisation that the people we were portraying on stage did not have that choice. The most we could offer them to ameliorate their pain was to use our performance to educate, enlighten, share, engender awareness amongst others or, at the very least, elicit compassion. In this respect, I hope our ragtag group from Southampton whose play seemed to coincide with the burgeoning general awareness of anorexia nervosa at that time justified Maureen's faith in us.

Sarah Blackman (Ensemble in the original production)

My confidence in what we were doing had already led me to pre-book the high profile Heriot Watt Theatre (Tic Toc Venues) for a week at the Edinburgh Fringe. I had such positive memories of our time up there with EYT and *Too Much Punch* in lesser (and considerably cheaper) venues and felt that there had to be a reward for such an intense process we faced which warranted far more than a mere three night run in our school. Remember at this time there was no play, just a belief that there would be! The whole thing was great in ambition but non-existent in substance! I hoped this would inspire something magical out of us all. There was no doubt. I had very high expectations. *Hard to Swallow* had to be good!

I imagine the success of *Too Much Punch for Judy* played a part in eliciting Maureen's permission, but I believe my reason for asking her permission in the first instance also played a significant part in her brave decision to trust me.

Photos: Ape Theatre Company

Chapter 2

Context and Inspiration for *Hard to Swallow*

Hard to Swallow is one of my most successful plays.

It has been published by two publishers, Cambridge University Press and dbda. CUP decided to discontinue the play when they downsized their catalogue in 1999. This was a surprising decision because, along with *Gregory's Girl*, I was given to understand that it was one of their best sellers.

I offered it, along with *Too Much Punch for Judy* (no one wanted to publish that despite it being incredibly popular!), to dbda (now Zinc Publishing), who had already published *Chicken!* with success. They took it on, but had reservations. As both plays had been published before they were fearful that the market may have already been fully exploited.

Despite their fears it has sold 26,765 copies (and is my second-best seller). *Too Much Punch* is about 7,000 ahead (at the time of writing July 2017).

Here are my Top 5 plays based on performances (September 2017). *Hard to Swallow* sneaks in at number 5!

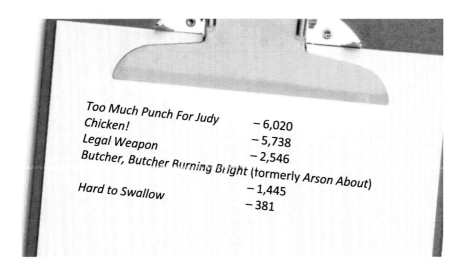

Too Much Punch For Judy — 6,020
Chicken! — 5,738
Legal Weapon — 2,546
Butcher, Butcher Burning Bright (formerly Arson About)
Hard to Swallow — 1,445
— 381

As a performance piece, the official statistics do not do it justice. I can only access statistics from licensed (royalty-bearing) performances. This doesn't include private (often exam) performances in school time with only school students and no parents in the audience.

It was selected, in 2016, as a set text on the first Eduqas GCSE 9-1 Drama specification (OCR selected *Missing Dan Nolan*). People ask whether I was expecting this. The answer is "absolutely not!" The two examination boards who selected my plays had never made any contact with me whatsoever. It was a total shock and I felt 'validated'! I was established as a 'popular playwright' in schools, mainly through the Edexcel (Pearson) exam board, so if I expected anything (and initially I didn't), I thought 'Pearson might'… but even that was an outside chance! Pearson were the last to announce their set text list. By then, I admit I had become hopeful and was disappointed they did not chose a play of mine.

1988-1990, when the play was conceived, were very different times. For me, it was a time when I started a new job at Oaklands Community School in Southampton, a job that I was to remain in for a further 29 years! They generously provided me with my first Word Processor, an Amstrad with a green screen monitor, though at this point I couldn't type well enough to write *Hard to Swallow* on it!

I would also buy my first house, get engaged and then married (to the long-suffering Rachael), have my first cat (Pussing), dog (Tillie), and finally baby boy (Ollie). So, for me, it was a period where I became a proper grown up!

Social, Cultural and Historical Context

In this era a number of significant events occurred which may help you to see the context in which we created this performance. Although I was a Drama teacher, mine was a pop/rock music(al) theatre background so, traditional classical theatre is something I neither appreciated nor knew much about. We were all learning on our feet and the professional productions I mention I saw (below) became my (and in turn the casts) main models for developing and honing our skillset.

- GCSEs replaced O Levels, CSEs and the trial 16+ exams. I remember the joy of the old CSE Drama courses that were 100% practical (those were the days!) There was suddenly a demand for students to use devising skills in performances of their own. I wanted to use OYT as a model for the way in which my students would achieve this.

  SNAP Theatre Company (from Hertfordshire) visit Oaklands and show us their imaginative staging of a TIE play. Their use of body-scenery was inspirational.

- We saw Trestle Theatre (masks) perform *Top Story*. Although what we were doing was very different, this made a huge impact on all of us and made us keen to ensure we had visual interest for the audience. It encouraged us to investigate the use of set for the first time.

- As a company we go to see the Hull Truck performance of John Godber's new play, *Teechers*. We acknowledge John's imaginative style of presentation (together with SNAP) as our main influence on our work. What was on the West End was impossible for us to emulate on our limited budget. Hull Truck (and SNAP's) work made professional standards seem possible. We felt our youth could bring additional zest to the performances.

- I also saw Cheek by Jowl's production of *Macbeth* (in Winchester) around this time. Once again, their performances were theatrically imaginative and ground-breaking. I remember the performers creating the sound of rain pitter-pattering on the stage floor with their fingernails. It was inexpensive magic! I approached OYT's storytelling with this as one of my models.

- My natural starting point is music rather than theatre... so... David Bowie (I have to mention him in anything I write!) stops being a solo artist and becomes the lead singer in Tin Machine. I bought the albums but was disappointed. Since his *The Next Day* album (which I love and reminded me of Tin Machine) I have come to like them a little more. When he disbands them he tours as a solo artist and plays a selection of songs ("for the last time", he said) selected by a vote from the British public. Despite *The Laughing Gnome* being a top selection he never performed it. I saw him at Milton Keynes Bowl with Ollie who was then 3 months old.

- Margaret Thatcher became Britain's first female Prime Minister but, by the end of this era, was suffering a dramatic fall from grace.

- Poll Tax Riots. I wasn't there but knew people who were. There were a series of protests in British towns and cities against Margaret Thatcher's Community Charge due to come into force in 1990. The biggest of these was in London on 31st March. Many believed this to signify the end of Thatcherism.

- Pan Am Flight 103 exploded over the Scottish town of Lockerbie, Dumfries and Galloway, killing a total of 270 people – 11 on the ground and all 259 on board. It was believed that the cause of the explosion was a terrorist bomb.

- 96 football fans were killed in the Hillsborough Disaster. All-seater stadiums became compulsory as a result. I remember hearing this unfolding live on the radio on my birthday as we were returning from a dog walk. We assumed/believed it to be "hooligans". Little did we know then, the shocking cover up to protect those in authority.

- *Falsettoland* opened off-Broadway and ran for 176 performances. I didn't see at the time but when I did, it became one of my favourite musicals. It is really worth checking this out! A musical about AIDS!

Anorexia in the 1980s

Anorexia was rarely, if ever, mentioned at this time. It had forced its way into my vocabulary when I was 20 (1978). Visiting my home town and trying to see Ann, an old friend from school, I discovered she had fainted on her doorstep weighing only 4 stone. She was not at home but was in hospital and was refusing to eat. Then anorexia was mentioned. I assumed it to be a very, very rare illness and vaguely remembered it being mentioned in association with a singer, Lena Zavaroni, a few years previously. As a lover of all things food, I could not relate to it at all! I never expected to hear of it again. (My full account of this, and Ann's story of a full recovery, appear in the Zinc Publishing (formerly dbda), *Hard to Swallow* script publication). I am pleased to report Ann is now fit, well and very positive.

Heading for my sixties, I am still free of something that felt like a constant ball and chain through years of my youth. I often look back and lament that I was at the mercy of an illness over which I had no control. If I were struggling nowadays with such an awful mental health condition I would seek out the wonderful therapies on offer, such as NLP, CBT and Mindfulness, which can assist so effectively in helping someone understand the causes for this self-punishment. Being helped to understand the reasons behind your illness empowers you to think positively and start to enjoy the gift of life that you've been given.

Ann

The next time I heard the word, was four years later (1983) when Karen Carpenter, a famous singer, died.

In 1986, a member of my (Epping) Youth Theatre came to me asking for advice. He thought his girlfriend was suffering from anorexia and asked me what he should do to help. He described how the doctor had told her to go away and see if she could put some weight on, before attending a follow-up appointment three weeks later! The best I could do was to put them in touch with my friend Ann, who was able to offer some useful advice. Jo has, I believe, made a full recovery. I decided to use her name "Jo" as the Goat, as a symbol of hope, on behalf of her and all those who have recovered (or are in recovery) from this dreadful syndrome.

It was then that I decided my next project would be a play about eating disorders. Anorexia Aid, who I had contacted regarding Jo, pointed me to Maureen's book, *Catherine*, that had been published a short while before. I read it and contacted Maureen to see if there was any possibility I could adapt it. I did this via letter through Anorexia Aid and soon afterwards, I received Maureen's positive reply.

Once I had decided to start this project, I visited the local Health Education Service. The Essex Health Education Service had given me invaluable support when I was developing *Quenchers* (the prototype for *Too Much Punch for Judy*). I went to the Southampton equivalent, expecting a similarly helpful response. I remember the shock of their reaction so well. On my return, I wrote this in my diary:

Diary

1/2/1988

Today I had a moment of realisation. Anorexia really is the ignored, yet ever more prevalent problem of our time. I had an appointment for the Health Education Department in Southampton. It transpires they have no books on anorexia, only five or six newspaper articles. They were embarrassed to admit that they had no policy or recognition of it, claiming that it was "too complex to deal with!"

"And drug abuse isn't?" I replied.

Something must be available for schools. Only three days ago I spotted someone with symptoms of anorexia, which without my interest, I would not have recognised and followed up. The play is now a necessity and will make an interesting and challenging project for OYT to premiere.

For the purposes of this book I asked the OYT cast what they knew about anorexia prior to their involvement in this play back in 1988. Here are some of their responses. It will give you some idea of the status of this condition prior to Princess Diana's game changing speech in 1993[4], five years after we started work on *Hard to Swallow*.

Anorexia was not talked about in 1988. I was aware of the suffragette movement, hunger strikes and forced feeding along with other cultures that ritually fasted, but I'd never come across anyone 'creating an issue' with food themselves when they weren't forced by circumstance to use food as some form of external protest.

I never liked the term "anorexia nervosa". It sounds cold, secretive and repelling. It doesn't engender sympathy like the names of other diseases do such as 'mumps'. "Nervosa" seemed to me like a catchall term used by men over the centuries to label women as 'hysterical' whenever they had no true understanding of the real issues at hand. The prototype-feminist in me found it quite dismissive.

The first time I heard anorexia being coupled with an actual person was when a tabloid ran a story (including photos) on the 'child star', Lena Zavaroni. My 9-year-old analysis of that article was this; only Lena knew what was really going on. Surely, had they known, managers, family and doctors would have successfully intervened. Something must have been seriously askew with her interpretation of her life because she was lauded as such a lucky and rare 'success story'.

"Anorexia", seemed, an incredibly rare and 'secret' disorder. Now social media portrays it as an elitist club, with people sharing tips on 'thinspiration' sites. I fear it's become fashionable/desirable. I remember thinking, what would have encouraged Catherine to choose this course of action? Had she thought it was unique to her and was following her own instincts?

Sarah Blackman (Ensemble in the original production)

---

[4] "Princess Diana's Speech on Eating Disorders" can be found on YouTube

I don't think I knew the term "eating disorder". I knew Lena Zavaroni had died from anorexia. I had no idea it was a psychological disorder.

Debra Giles

I don't recall knowing anything about it. The difference from then and now is huge. When we first started to talk about it in OYT I think I would have considered it a "girl thing" only.

Richard Brown

Awareness of eating disorders and how to treat sufferers was woefully inadequate.

Chris Vaudin

Catherine – Picture from Mark's *Hard to Swallow* scrapbook

Chapter 3

Rehearsals and Preparation Period

> *The process of writing a play about such a sensitive subject as anorexia, based on a true and tragic story, was truly educational. In speaking directly to Maureen Dunbar, we were granted unmediated access to her recollections of her daughter's illness and the impact it had on their entire family. This gave our close-knit ensemble a huge sense of responsibility: the story needed to be told with honesty and clarity. I began, even at the tender age of 14, to gain a deep-seated belief in the power of theatre to communicate a powerful message to its audience.*

Chris Vaudin (Baby Goat and Double Yellow line!)

My first big move in the development of the initial OYT production came three days after my visit to the Health Education Centre. What I did risked alienating the stability of the group I had chosen to work with...but still I went ahead and did it! This is typical of my way of working...my attitude was – 'It seems like a good idea. Yeah, let's risk it!'

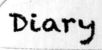

Diary   4/2/88

The production has really moved forward tonight. I have stepped into the unknown and cast Catherine. She is someone I don't know and hadn't met until this evening. She has an amazing opportunity and must take it.

Two weeks ago, Rachael (my then girlfriend and now wife) said to me to cast Catherine from outside the group... someone to be 'new on the scene'.

"Who?" I replied.

Diary

... "Someone no-one in the group knows in a drama context... someone plucked out of the crowd."

"Who?"

"Well... there is this girl at the Youth Club (where Rachael worked)... pop in tonight and take a look."

So, I did, while the HTS cast were working on a documentary style version of Red Riding Hood to help prepare them for dealing with the approach we were to take with Catherine's story.

I walked over to the Youth Club (also on the Oaklands site) saw Rach and immediately spotted a girl playing Patience on her own, noticeably serene among this group. Confident, assured and upright... very upright, unmistakably someone I felt who would have the aura I saw as a key quality our "Catherine" needed.

"Is that the girl you were talking about?"

"Yes. Her name is Abigail."

She had no idea who I was and I admit being frightened of a rebuff as I approached her to ask.

Diary

Within 20 minutes her Mum was there, discussing the commitment and all was agreed. Abigail was our Catherine.

This is a very exciting casting. She will stand out and be so different.

When I informed the group, later, I knew I must contain my excitement. I didn't want to cause any offence.

Their Red Riding Hood devised pieces were staggeringly good! Then I had to make the announcement: "I have some awkward news to bring. When Maureen was here, I looked around and couldn't really see a 'Catherine'. I know some of you may have been hoping to play this role. Well... earlier this evening I have to tell you I cast that role."

Richard Brown interrupted. "Oh! Disappointing!" (He was implying, in jest, that he had seen himself as being in line for the part.)

His comment was perfect to break the tension. Everyone seemed to accept the news with good faith and good cheer. I hope that's the case anyway!

One of the cast confided in me that she thought I had my girlfriend in line for the part, so hadn't thought any of them would be playing Catherine anyway!

Abigail is Catherine.

We are in for a BIG success!

I knew nothing about this girl! She hadn't opted for Drama so I had no idea if she could act. All I had was a hunch... and commitment to the fact that we would make it work. From everything I discovered in those early moments I became aware she was very different to everyone else. She had clear aspirations. She wanted to become a lawyer. She was going to have to balance this commitment carefully alongside her desire for impeccable grades. It was in retrospect a leap of faith (for Abigail as well as us)... like so much of what I do. A leap of faith... just like the one Maureen had made towards us!

Richard Brown remembers the casting as being a complete surprise.

I was shocked. Abigail was in my class. I didn't really have time for her and neither did my circle of friends. I never thought it would work and was not happy. She turned out to be a star and a real asset to the group. She loved being part of this group and it seemed to give her so much as a person. We became friends and my whole perspective and openness to others who I would not previously associate with developed. OYT really helped me to grow up.

From a female perspective, Sarah's recollections, which arrived in my inbox after I'd written the above, made me laugh out loud!!!

I don't remember us discussing this during rehearsals, which sounds odd! We were all assuming that it would happen organically or Mark would get around to it in his own sweet time. We had been working together for a few months and had forged effective and good humoured working relationships with each other.

Then, completely out of the blue, Mark made an announcement. Correction, it wasn't an announcement, it was a declaration!
He stood halfway up the bank of theatre seating (out of arms reach?!) and 'sermon on the mount' style bellowed down to us that he had "found his Catherine".

It all sounded a little bit Svengali-esque to me. Weren't we good enough or were we merely worker bees, toiling away in preparation for the Queen Bee's arrival? I half expected this new 'muse' of Mark's to descend from the sky on a cloud to the sound of harps!

Possibly noses were momentarily put out of joint amongst the female cast members (we didn't actually discuss this at the time as we were so utterly engrossed in building the play as a whole).

In a way, it made perfect sense that the person playing Catherine would come from a different source than the rest of us.

Bringing in an 'outsider' at this stage was symbolic of Catherine's isolation from everyone else.

> *Abigail, when she arrived, didn't descend from a cloud. She was tall, brunette and willowy, one of those young women with seemingly longer and more elegant limbs than most, two of which she walked on to the next rehearsal where we could all meet her and acknowledge more than a passing physical resemblance to the real Catherine, and a voice without the Hampshire brogue that most of us had.*
>
> *I wonder, in hindsight, if Mark's casting choice was the first time we were confronted with the idea of body image as a factor between 'us'. Why, when as performers we played everything from fridge freezers, Billy Goats and moving vehicles, had Mark made this decision to cast the central character based so much upon appearance?*

Sarah Blackman (Ensemble in the original production)

It's heart-warming to read the shock this, seemingly out of character, autocratic diktat had. I'm proud that, even after such a short amount of time, it proved to be totally against their expectations of me. I like to keep my cast on their toes with little surprises here and there! Abigail benefitted our first production more than I could have hoped for. I am delighted to say that she fulfilled the ambition she held at that time; to be a criminal barrister, an outstanding achievement for a girl living on the much maligned Lordshill estate.

The challenges of a play about anorexia

Things weren't always rosy. No one should think developing this play was a walk in the park.

Diary 21/2/88

Yesterday evening I very nearly backed out. The morbidity of the subject matter was beginning to haunt/frighten me. I feel responsible forcing these young people from doing too deep an analysis into what is, I now realise, a "mental illness." It could be disturbing for them. I am concerned as to how such a story of someone's failure to overcome this problem can possibly work as an inspiration to those who watch it.

Rachael was angry I had not fully considered this previously. We talked and eventually she brought me round to a more positive viewpoint.

There was some anxiety from parents too. I remember Abigail's father coming to see me, wanting to know why I had chosen this subject. He was reassured by my answer, (I imagine talking about Ann and Jo) but said he would have preferred the play to be about something else.

Diary 22/2/88

Maybe we will deviate from the documentary approach. I am keen to "use" Deanne's (the sole older (18) experienced cast member by this point) imaginative/intelligent staging ideas and also the vital comedy Sarah Blackman brings to it. These will offer contrasts to the more static documentary approach I have taken in the past.

I am feeling much more optimistic about it all and excited about all the possibilities it might offer.

I think this was me starting, consciously, to use the more physical approach that the OYT-production of Race to Be *Seen* had taken. Physical Theatre was a term I'd never, at that time, heard.

Capturing Catherine's story

I never had any doubt that the best way to tell this story was to use the words of Catherine and her family. This approach had worked well in both *Race* and *Too Much Punch*. I was keen to build on the success and quality they had achieved and the reception that had greeted both. Maureen's book, *Catherine*, provided me with all the research I would need in one volume. It featured:

- a commentary on events by Maureen
- diary entries written by Catherine
- chapters written by her brothers (in the play I decided to merge them to become one person)
- a chapter detailing John, her father's recollections and deep regret about his part in the situation.

I didn't need to interview Catherine's family, so I didn't meet any of them at this point. This was a contrast to my previous projects where I had conducted in depth interviews with the real people, come to know them well and maintained regular contact throughout the rehearsal period. There was also a geographical distance between us. I was keen not to become intrusive so never pressed for more words or any additional interviews. I was given Catherine's diaries so may well have included extra words in the play from this very private resource.

As a writer, with a couple of minor successes behind me, the tag of being a 'teacher/playwright' had started to give me a little more confidence but I had also begun to feel like a bit of a fraud. Arranging other peoples' words seemed more like 'editing' than 'playwriting'. Having only achieved a CSE Grade 2 in English Lit and a Grade 1 in English at school (equivalent to Grades 3 & 4 in the 9-1 GCSE exams) I didn't have an ingrained confidence in my own writing skills. I concluded that I should use this play to prove I could write 'proper plays'. So, I used *Hard to Swallow* to invent words and prove myself as a writer alongside my already proven documentary playwriting/editing skills.

For the Brussels Sprouts scene, I went as far as to fake the documentary approach. Maureen told me this story when we visited her to show her an early (incredibly long) draft of the play. I remember thinking this could, if staged with lots of body scenery, offer a rare moment of comedy leading to the hard-hitting climax. 'We must use this', I thought, but I had no tape recorder to record Maureen's words. So, when I got home that night, I wrote it down from memory as though I was Maureen. She has never commented on it so I must have done a pretty good job!!! When I gave the scene to the cast to develop into a physical scene, they loved it!

> *I remember developing one scene where we had to simulate a car! This was brand new to me. We realised that scenery and props weren't imperative. We could use our bodies and be even more creative.*

Donna Batt (Cast ensemble)

I remember developing family argument scenes using a technique I'd first used in scripting my musical, *Blackout* (about the evacuation in WW2). Workshop groups improvised the scenes based on the outline given by Maureen in her book. I would make notes from these improvised scenes and also get the cast to write them up. Then, at home, I used those ideas to inspire a "next stage' script, mixing in material from the book.

Hard to Swallow also contains the first dialogue scene I wrote on my own, in which Catherine and Anna battle over the scales. I remember lying on my front room floor inventing this, and struggling over it for ages, trying to make it sound 'real'. I am certain that, once I heard the performers acting it out, it went through further developments as various parts still didn't sound right. This always happens with my scripts... changes throughout rehearsals... constantly!!!

I made contact with a local psychotherapist, Tony Saunders, who worked with anorexics. He became an 'expert' advisor to the project. He looked at my early drafts and offered many developments/corrections. He allowed me to witness a Family Therapy exercise, which was subsequently used with the "family" in our cast, enabling them to gain a better understanding of the familial relationships. This led to an image that would, much later, appear in the Sunday Times Colour Supplement!

OAKLANDS YOUTH THEATRE *'This has given us loads of ideas'*

Family Therapy Exercise

The family group have to make three family pictures for a (formal) photographer, using the Drama technique of still imaging or tableaux.
They justify their chosen positions in relation to the other family members in each picture. They discuss their thoughts as they prepare for each photograph.
1. The Dunbar family prior to Catherine's illness
2. The Dunbar family at the onset of Catherine's illness
3. The Dunbar family towards the end of Catherine's illness

Once the three images are created, they perform each one, morphing, over a count of 10, from one picture to the next and trying to feel what their character is feeling during the transitions.

Each individual then shares:
• what they discovered about their role
• what they observed in any of the other people

Finally, without any discussion, Catherine is removed from the image (representing her passing). How does this affect the positioning of the remaining people and their inter-relations?

Once settled in a final position there will be a period of discussion.

This proved a memorable exercise and one that we would often refer to later on in our "interesting" development and rehearsal process.

'From the ground up', 'from the wall inwards' 'from the ceiling down', I think all of these terms can be used to describe the process of devising theatre! Gone is the script that has been set in stone for however many years. Gone are the preordained entrances and exits. Gone is the version you watched last year to make sense of the script and borrowing ideas, like a thespian magpie. Gone are the scholar's notes and the chance for comparison and critical reviews from countless past interpretations. Here we were, creating all of the above for ourselves, from thin air, supported by the facts, events and memories given by people entrusting us with a very public demonstration of their very private lives. 'Hard to Swallow' felt like a 'Ben Hur' of a production!

The research period included interviews with recovering anorexics alongside doctors and psychologists treating them at that time. This proved invaluable in trying to understand the landscape from 'inside' an anorexic's mind.

In an effort to shift the group from a child's perspective (Catherine and her siblings) to that of the adults (her parents, teachers and carers) we improvised situations dealing with loss, responsibility and familial relationships.

I remember one where I played a mother on the evening her son was leaving to join a military conflict. I don't consider myself maternal. I am childless by choice, but I still remember the excruciating ache that descended on me when he finally had to leave. I recall the silence in the theatre and the chasm it left between the two of us. Whilst momentarily sobered by the experience of embodying a parent's physical loss I would still continue to go about my own life afterwards, unaffected. That exercise brought home to me how a parent suffering loss, could not. For the first time I felt I had got into Maureen and John's shoes so to speak!

'Hard to Swallow' became a play which fused naturalistic dialogue and physically stylistic scenes to highlight a point or re-create an event in a more imaginative way than purely reciting it. As powerful and invaluable as each person's personal account was, we were determined our version of this story would not become a series of monologues.

Maintaining a suitable pace and showing the varied dynamics between Catherine and other characters was crucial. Scenes were interspersed with, and offset against, Catherine's diary entries. These "solo' diary moments acted as a symbolic device to show her dependence on them, their secretive nature, and the regulated and repetitive actions that form part of anorexia itself.

It wasn't until much later, when we had the semblance of a script that those of us not playing a family member knew what roles we would play. The casting was a mix of logistics from one scene to the next, and a person's suitability (or not) to necessary characteristics. By the time we cast it, and I think we did, rather than Mark did, most people had already played most characters. At one stage I developed a scene as Catherine's father!

In the beginning stages I had no idea what it would end up looking like. I'd like to think Mark had that covered! (I didn't!) *When devising, we worked on disparate scenes until the skeleton of the play began to emerge. Mark set the task, disappeared to the bar (for an orange juice – his tipple of choice) and returned after 40 minutes to "see what we'd come up with".*

The beauty of devising in a team is that an individual's personal strengths come to the fore. The theorists and writers enjoy the editing process and filling in the missing parts of a scene. The activists in the group enjoy the role-playing, and physically testing out, not only the text, but the emotional content of each scene. Everyone has the chance to play director and give feedback.

Sarah Blackman (Ensemble cast)[5]

My diary over the next month indicates that the subject matter I had chosen continued to be controversial for me, in a school more used to light-hearted productions.

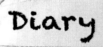

Diary   24/2/88

I think this may mark my final 'issue play'. I will move back to large

scale community musicals. I don't like the tensions this produces inside

me – should I? Shouldn't I? I am sure these feelings will only intensify

leading up to the in-house performances in June.

---

[5] Yes! Our progressive school even had a bar that was always open in the evenings! It made an excellent onsite venue for post rehearsals to continue.

Diary

Maureen, who visited yesterday (bringing with her pictures, and diaries), has put her Trust fund's money behind it, to the tune of £500 (equivalent to about £1,300 in 2017)!

She seemed really pleased with my outline scenario. This has really renewed my somewhat flagging confidence as I don't think adults here (teachers etc.) understand what we're doing – or why. There are a few notable exceptions. Most would rather we were doing a pantomime!

Diary

We had a much-needed BRILLIANT meeting on Thursday. Debbie, Sharon, Chris and Richard came up with a brilliant Billy Goat story - "The Grass Is Always Greener on the Other Side". It was beautiful, simple and so appropriate.

We have about 1/16th of the play completed! Argh. I am struggling to keep up with this and the huge amount of marking I have as I am also a Humanities teacher this year!

We need to get a move on!

Those Billy Goats!

> *Suddenly we had the freedom to explore and experiment with what was, to me, a new kind of drama/theatre. It wasn't just reading a script or being directed, we were given opportunities to share ideas with other students and the teacher. It was collaborative. I remember vividly a section in the play that refers to billy goats crossing a bridge. I never thought a production about anorexia could contain humour or metaphors.*

Donna Batt (Jo the Goat/Ensemble cast)

Teachers, directors and students studying the play often contact me to ask about the Billy Goats scenes. 'Why did you include Billy Goats?' Some even dare to ask if they can cut them! Cut them??? Noooo!

On the 10th March 1988, a hugely significant invention was made by some of the younger members of OYT. It would offer a way to have the optimistic ending I had been looking for!

It is perhaps that I love this kind of children's story and that linked well to the idea of an anorexic regressing to childhood. More importantly and on a practical level, I felt it was crucial for the play to have an attention-grabbing opening. A scene about Billy Goats would certainly not be what an audience would expect from a play about anorexia and the surprise would make the audience focus! I was keen to throw the audience off balance! Once it was in our minds to include such a story, we went to town.

Today, I looked at the original hand written draft of the play for the first time in 30 years. There are fifteen pages (about 30 minutes) of Billy Goat scenes. They are surprisingly beautiful! The scenes in this original (handwritten) draft, occur at key moments in Catherine's story and reflect or foreshadow these events[6].

It is interesting to note that the original scenes refer to the field at the other side of the bridge as "enchanted", and having "beautiful flowers".

At one point, Baby brings home sparkling rocks in an attempt to make his feuding parents happier. It was important that Baby was male, to show anorexia is not a female preserve. However, once in their home, the sparkle fades.

The Troll's rhyme had a food related twist:

> *"I am the troll and this is my bridge. If you dare to pass you'll be in my fridge!"*

The playpen was originally a "tiny maze", built by Baby to take his mind off the dangers of the ugly troll. Baby was contented in it because, unlike other mazes, he had mastered this one and could

---

[6] Available from www.resources4drama.co.uk Crossing the Bridge – The Unseen Billy Goat scenes from Hard to Swallow.

never get lost in it. The maze was, over time, protected by an increasing number of doors Baby erects, preventing others from gaining access.

In the penultimate Billy Goat scene, Baby leaves the maze but on his return discovers the troll has broken in. The troll chases Baby up the jagged mountain, beneath which is an Ocean. We presume he jumps.

In the final, climatic scene, Jo the Goat visits Baby's field and is taken into the maze by the spirit of Baby. The final door to Baby's maze is locked. Baby hurled the key away, so when they arrive at the entrance they are only able to peer through a window. Guess what they see inside? "The flickering image of a tiny and very ugly troll".

Jo the Goat returns to her field and dismantles the maze she was building and, with the troll trapped in Baby's maze, she remains free to play happily ever after in her field!

Awwwww!

In the week of the first performance we did a run through and discovered the play was far too long. We were all thinking 'What do we cut?'

This wasn't a simple matter of cutting lines. It also meant we would have to cut roles. I had to be autocratic again (responsibilities of a leader)! We needed to shed about 30 minutes.

> *Right… Chris, Sharon etc. Go into the theatre while we look at the main body of the play. Can you work on reducing the Billy Goats scenes to one single scene lasting about five minutes!*

I don't remember any arguments. They just went and, using the same technique we used to reduce the ritual of Catherine visiting the hospital repeatedly over a few years, into a few minutes (what I call precis, or Two Touch theatre[7]), this little group cut the Billy Goats into pretty much the scenes that appear in the script today.

I didn't worry that it had lost a lot of the beauty, something had to give! It had solved our problem fast and was entertaining. The group had been clever and we let them know they'd rescued us!

We all knew this would make a great beginning to the play… and then… if we reprised the scene at the end it would be… and if we mixed Patricia into it… oooh and John… oooh and Maureen. Wow!

That is how it came to be. No grand master plan. One idea led to another organically! We had a problem; we solved it. Some young people must have lost a major role but no one (in my memory) ever complained. We were all relieved that whatever the problem there was also a resolution… and often, it provided us with a more imaginative outcome! There was a general understanding that these personal sacrifices were for the good of the production. That over-rode everything for

---

[7] Precis Theatre is described in detail in my The Story Behind Too Much Punch For Judy book (Pping Publishing 2013)

all of us. This example, crystallises my memory of the generous modus operandi we always operated within OYT.

> *I really enjoyed this collaborative approach. If we hit a wall or dropped the baton, there were others to pick it up and get it moving again. There was a tangible sense of creativity and freedom, including blind alleys, dead ends and going round and round in circles.*
>
> *Sometimes we came up with nubs of ideas but we also became conversant with returns to the drawing board! We experienced ideas being rejected if decided against by the team. This was such an important lesson in ego, letting go and moving on. There were also lessons in embellishing other people's ideas and moving them in a different direction from their original intention. Those Billy Goats didn't just appear out of thin air!*

Sarah Blackman

The Billy Goats are so important in this telling of Maureen's story. They:

- establish the style of performance with the narrative/precis theatre and imaginative staging
- offer a rare opportunity for liveliness, and comedy
- put the audience off balance by starting the play with unexpected content
- are initially incomprehensible but by the end of the play, when the scene is reprised so, in true TIE style, the audience become aware of what they have learnt because the reprised version, makes complete sense, given the now known context of the Dunbar's experience. It also enables the play to end with a positive and upbeat message of hope.

So… please, please don't cut the Billy Goats but see them as an opportunity for all the above! We continued to work unbelievably hard. I recorded four days on the trot in the Easter holidays, working with the whole cast from 10am – 6pm to complete the initial draft of the play! I have to admit vacillating between being glad to have made the move to Southampton and missing my old, more experienced, Epping Youth Theatre cast.

On 31st March I reported that:

The following day I worked on it for 15 hours pretty much non-stop, developing the Goat scenes, little knowing they would all be cut!!!

Early rehearsals

Diary

The read-through of my edited script was painfully slow and really pointed out the boring bits. It was difficult to become involved in the story because there was so much retrospective, narrative speech. In rehearsals, we will have to spice it up significantly and it needs serious editing!

The cast are finding the Billy Goat scenes difficult to handle bar Deanne who keeps saying 'They're good. They'll lighten it up a bit.'

Most are not committed to them, which is likely to make them fail. Big worry! I need to look at some these narrative scenes and make them work. We need to work on making it visually impressive as well.

28/4/1988

I have made a rule. No scene should be static!

23/5/1988

Our lighting people have all dropped out!

Kalwant has stepped in which will, I hope be a good thing. Gary keeps saying he will drop out but at the moment seems determined to remain. Rehearsals are frighteningly slow. I am rewriting more than anything I've ever done before. I'm pleased with our use of music (Carpenters). We are going to have to work really hard to make this come off.

Diary

25/5/88

After yesterday night's rehearsal, I feel like giving up. It isn't working. I want to do it but feel it isn't saying the right thing. The acting is appalling, except for Richard, who oozes life and projection. Apart from him it's boring, slow and lacks clarity.

Diary

25/5/88

Once again, I question the documentary techniques that I claim to believe in so fully!

27/6/88

I have recruited a college student, Andy Stott to play John, in place of Jason, who has had to drop out. Andy has brought up the standard of our performance in leaps and bounds. Although I felt threatened by his confidence at first, I feel comfortable with him now. He is full of imaginative ideas and has worked well with me to develop the play beyond recognition.

... Chris has continued to be a tower of strength. Debbie is very

impressive, as are Abigail and Deanne. Richard is being a bit

disappointing. Gary is now working really hard.

... and that is where my diary suddenly comes to a halt. I think I was just too busy to write it and felt that it was probably repetitive of the ones I'd written for Punch or Race... after all, being realistic, would I ever have any reason to look at them again? They seemed likely to be a complete waste of my precious time. Looking back, it's a shame because they have been so useful to bring this period back to life.

The insight I get into the 30-year-old Mark Wheeller is to witness an anxious guy, keen to impress in a new job, hoping that something, somewhere, will rescue him but having no control over what that would be or if indeed it might happen.

That rescue arrived, out of the blue, from Andrew, from Basingstoke. (I remember nothing more about how he came to become involved and have totally lost contact with him since he left OYT) but he was a step above all of us in terms of experience and we benefitted from him immensely. Other than Deanne, he was, and seemed, much older and more experienced than us (me included). I was surprised he chose to stay in what was a young group... but he did... at least for the time being.

Coming off the back of an award-winning TV film and successful book we picked up a lot of local publicity for the play. The papers were particularly interested when Maureen came to visit us in rehearsals or if we visited her at her home. This generated a really positive feeling between all of us. We felt we were doing something very special right from the outset.

> *It was strange standing in the same house that Catherine had lived in. Her mum was lovely to me and played me tapes Catherine had made. I have more insight into anorexia now but cannot say I understand it. Since we started the play I have become more aware of food and have begun to eat more healthily. In playing Catherine I merely provide the body for Catherine's mind. She is like two people. Half of her is caring and the other half is like a monster when the anorexia takes control.*

Abigail Penny (1988, from a newspaper interview)

It was fascinating for me to visit Maureen's flat (2017) a few weeks ago and see, all these years later, she still had framed photos of the production we presented to her in pride of place, amongst those of her own children. It is clear this also mattered very much to Maureen. That was lovely to see.

By the time we came to perform the first version of the play, then entitled simply *"Catherine"*, we knew Maureen was clearly with us and offered her unconditional support.

We were acutely aware of the responsibility we had to Maureen, initially as an individual but now as a friend, to portray her daughter and the whole family situation appropriately. We were, I hope, particularly sensitive to the sharp contrast between our feelings of excitement about presenting this new play and the pain and sadness it would kindle in Maureen as she watched our dramatisation at our first performances on July 7th 1988. Preparations were going very well and people in the school were… well… intrigued, is I guess the best description. It was gathering a tremendous head of steam… and interest. The Times Educational Supplement had booked in to review an early performance so it was going national and this review would be hugely important to our publicity for the Edinburgh Festival Fringe. The pressure was on and the production was beginning to take shape.

One area where we had an unexpected and very high quality input was with the set design. I have never had any idea about set which is why my previous plays never had any! Suddenly, after two terms of being at Oaklands I heard that my predecessor, Paul Harris, had been appointed to an English post in the school and was returning. You can imagine, I had mixed feelings about this. I was just getting my feet under the table and was a bit suspicious that, in truth, what he wanted was his job back!!!

He was actually very sensitive to me, particularly as Drama was being "done" very differently now. He expressed open enthusiasm to voluntarily assist with the Youth Theatre. After discovering I had no ability with set design, he offered to take that on completely! He was an absolute godsend. He was probably one of the first people to see our work in progress and, despite us only being able to show a tiny fragment of the play, he was knocked out by what we had done… or what we were trying to do. The only restriction I made was that the set must be easy to fit into a van and tour.

A few days later Paul presented his set design. I can't imagine how we were rehearsing without one! His idea was, for the first time in one of my plays, a decent balance of being artistic and practical and much more than my normal "black empty space" with perhaps a raised area!

The Set

Downstage left was a fold-down meal table in light pine wood. When the leaves were folded down it was slim enough to fit into a car boot. On stage, we angled the table diagonally and surrounded it with 5 fold up chairs. It was hardly the grand dining table Catherine's family would have had but it offered a clear indication of family life and symbol of mealtime. Each place on the table was laid with cutlery and (innocent) white crockery. Under the table was (what we felt looked like) a quality rug which offered an indication of luxury and homeliness.

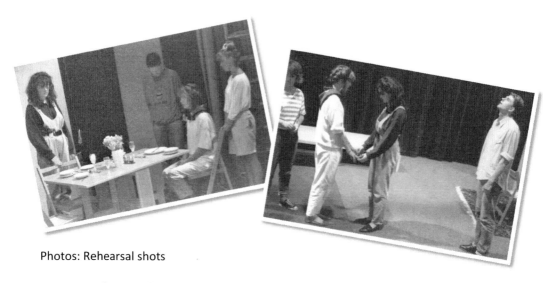

Photos: Rehearsal shots

Upstage and across the middle was a raised area, painted (innocent) white, about 0.5m high and 3m long by 1m deep. We used this area often for characters with status, for example the doctors who deliver speeches during the binge; and to represent the bridge in the Billy Goats scene. There was a stretch of red (danger?) carpet coming forward from the middle of the raised area to give a loose impression of a catwalk (we used it as such in an early version of the play with a short dance to the Sparks song "Looks Looks Looks"). We were keen to add a nod to the fashion industry which, it was felt by the cast, had more than a passing responsibility for this syndrome. Interestingly, it was something Catherine's family didn't want to be highlighted too much as they felt it wasn't a factor in her story.

Downstage right we had Catherine's bedroom desk (the space underneath doubled as Baby's playpen) with lots of "girl stuff" on the table. It was the area Catherine always sat in when she presented extracts from her diary. I remember buying this from MFI. It was easy to dismantle and so easy to tour. It was a light grey with red legs and edging to the table so was suitably colour coordinated with the other components in the set. Catherine had a red fold up chair to sit on by the desk. This was placed facing the audience directly … perhaps the most vulnerable placement we could consider for Catherine to direct address her diary entries. I remember I placed Maureen at Catherine's desk when she makes her final speech about Catherine, during the final Billy Goat scene.

We had a huge cinema screen in our well-equipped theatre which we could pull down to show the slides above and behind the cast. In other venues we ended up putting a simple stand up portable screen beside Catherine's bedroom DSR (or if there was no room we resolved the problem by walking on with the screen for the scene and moving it once it had been used).

Our theatre was a modern 165 seater studio theatre. It was end-on but there was no proscenium arch. We did the performance in some pros. arch locations but I preferred it to be open and was never concerned if there was no 'wing' area. The cast were very good at being neutral and sitting there focussing their (and therefore the audience's) attention on the play. The audience soon became immune to their presence. Their discipline was exceptional!

40

There were many occasions we performed without any lighting. It was crucial that the lighting was only there to support and enhance. The performers had to focus the audience and always make the play sufficiently interesting to hold the audience's attention. Holding the audience's attention is crucial! I always see my work through my own 14 year-old eyes. Had I picked up one of my scripts, at 14, I would have put it down straight away, being put off by the long sections of unbroken speech. Fortunately, people who see my plays on stage don't suffer from this because the physical performances compensate for it. Students in school are a different matter. They often see the script first!

Performance styles?

I am often asked if my approach would be Brecht or Stanislavski? My work rarely fits into these neat 'boxes' across a whole play. When I wrote *Hard to Swallow* I would have had a very basic knowledge of these practitioners though I would have been aware that the roots of Documentary Theatre[8] lie clearly with Brecht.

However, I would suggest there are scenes where a Stanislavskian approach comes to the fore.

I wanted the binge scene to be horribly real. Catherine had to eat the most bizarre mix of food in a crazed manner, wiping it around her mouth and messing herself with the food. It needed to look disgusting. I was never happy with this unless there were involuntary noises (there were) from the audience as they watched!

> *The binge scene was extremely powerful, underscored by an eerie music box sound. Catherine piled a mix of foods into her mouth, smothering yogurt and food over her face. I remember watching the audiences' faces and could see the effect this powerful scene had on them.*

Donna Batt (Ensemble cast)

In contrast, the scene where Maureen shows slides taken of Catherine when she was only 3-4 stone offers a perfect example of the alienation effect. This often caused the audience to react with involuntary gasps of horror! Despite 'Catherine' the actor being on stage, images of the real Catherine appear on a screen behind her. Somehow, this seems to make the audience believe even more in the portrayal of our actor playing Catherine. It is a totally honest approach, as though she's saying:

That's the real Catherine. I'm just here representing her.

---

[8] I offer a more detailed history of Documentary/Verbatim Theatre in *The Story Behind Too Much Punch for Judy* by Mark Wheeller (Pping Publishing 2013)

There are scenes of dialogue where I really wanted the cast to fully inhabit their characters. There is a section where the cast are treated as puppets and are merely representing their characters in a very obvious manner, while being manipulated by the ensemble. There is a moment where a character (the psychotherapist) appears as a superhero. This would be neither Brecht nor Stanislavski, it would be 'cartoon'! There would be nothing I would like more than the Billy Goats to have an element of Disney about them. I have always wanted *Hard to Swallow* to be a fusion of all sorts of textures and styles. The more the merrier!

The Romsey School production, directed by Ali Clarke, has been produced for the official Wheellerplays DVD. The performers use Frantic Assembly as their inspiration. They were founded in 1994, so we didn't have them as a possible model back then!

Characterisation

My decision about how we should present Catherine was hugely significant. I wanted her to appear noticeably 'different', and wanted to avoid the potentially dangerous feeling that I must cast her with an unusually thin actress. To achieve this freedom, I suggested we paint her face white, like the stock Pierrot pantomime character (which I had become aware of via David Bowie in the Ashes to Ashes video) and use a music box sound with gnomic horror voices (again used often by Bowie to create a spooky effect in his songs eg. After All) to underscore her diary entries.[9].

If Catherine had a significant journey to make she moved in a robotic style to convey "difference" using the same music box underscore. An example of this was when Simon meets her at the station and barely recognises her.

Zara Barnes from the 10th anniversary OYT production

I am often asked about characterisation. The central characters in this play aren't "characters", they are real people.

Most people who perform this play won't know the real person, so any attempt to impersonate them goes out of the window. In any case, they will only be known as real people to a few, if any, of the audience. I wouldn't want people gauging the success of a performance on the accuracy of the impersonation.

---

[9] We used Steve Harley and Cockney Rebel's *Innocence and Guilt* (before the vocal comes in).

I do very little characterisation work with my casts. We tend to explore how each performer might try to make the person they are playing come to life by using elements of their own personal experience appropriate to the particular scene. I ask them to bring their reality to the person's words.

I would hate there to be any hint of "fake" to any performance. The instruction I wrote in the introduction to the first dbda script in 2000 still stands so, I repeat it here once again:

> *It must at all times be remembered when reading or performing this play that the events portrayed are as close to the truth as memory will allow. The performers should not impersonate the real-life characters but breathe a life into them that is a reasonable interpretation of the words in the book. The actors should avoid overstatement and should veer towards underplaying. You can trust the material... you really can. It is, after all, as close as possible to the real thing.*

Re-reading this I will raise a slight question about my saying "veer towards underplaying." I have since seen performances where a clearer, more outward expression of emotions has been incredibly effective, and a Frantic style movement has been a part of this expressive portrayal. I think what, in retrospect, I was trying to say was that in the family scenes, please avoid any sense of melodrama.

July 7th finally arrived. The poster, designed by Epping Youth Theatre's John Rowley, (the final one he would do for me before we discovered our own home grown talent in Southampton) pulled no punches and gave a clear indication of our intentions.

We felt we were (nearly) ready, though, as ever, an extra week to prepare would have been welcome. It was being talked about in the community and tickets were selling well.

What would people think?

How would Maureen react with an audience there?

We were incredibly nervous.

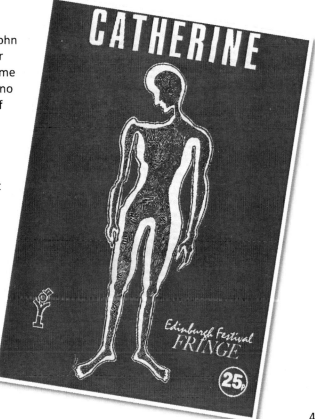

We needed good reviews to be assured of selling any tickets at the Fringe.

Were these inexperienced 'rag-tags' from Southampton really up to it?

Chapter 4

Preview and Premiere Performances

The whole project was ever evolving. The gathering of momentum was tangible. We spent quite a bit of time squashed into our school minibus along with the set and stage blocks on the way to performances in all sorts of venues and locations. Opportunities seemed to spring up left, right and centre. I can still taste the electric atmosphere we had around us at times; reviews, competitions, TV/radio coverage and press interviews. We'd settled on a gold standard of performance but we maintained a sense of variation and freshness about it.

The audience tended not just to pick up their coats and leave the auditorium after a performance! They loitered with intent! We met many interesting people from all walks of life that wanted to converse and share their views on the subject and listen to our interpretation of it. They were the type of people it may have taken us 5 – 10 years to stumble upon in our 'normal lives'. This was incredibly bolstering for me as a teen. OYT took us from a small circle of experience into a much wider circle both on and off stage. I often felt part of a phenomenon... not just a Youth Theatre, such was our timing with the anorexia zeitgeist at the time.

Sarah Blackman (Ensemble cast in the original production)

David Bowie often talks about his coke habit leading to him forgetting everything about the time in his life when he was recording Station to Station. He was about the same age as me when I was working on Hard to Swallow. I didn't have a coke habit. I have never done drugs, have barely even drunk alcohol but I still can't remember much detail about working towards this project. Sadly, I remember nothing about those first performances nor the detail of how they were received. I had completely forgotten some of the venues we had performed in. I have photographs, adverts, newspaper reviews/cuttings and some correspondence to jog my memory. It is only by using this that I shall try to pick the narrative of what happened and augment this with the casts' better memories.

The Hampshire Drama Advisor, Alistair Black came to see it on the first preview night and wrote a complimentary letter to our Head, Pete Hollis, the following day. It obviously hadn't gone badly!

> Please convey my thanks and congratulations to everyone involved in the production of Catherine... Everyone must be very proud to be associated with the production which dealt so sensitively and imaginatively with a very complex and difficult subject. I am delighted that they will be taking it to the Edinburgh Festival Fringe.
> I am sure Catherine would have been very pleased with the way you portrayed her life and also the way you give hope to other sufferers of Anorexia.

Maureen had given us her seal of approval, wholeheartedly. A comment she made at the time went on to be part of our Edinburgh hand-out.

> This play moved me to tears. I hope it will remove the guilt of those who do not have the power to change.

We also had another seal of approval, from Rev Pauline Newton from Anorexia Aid, who had originally helped put me in touch with Maureen. They attended in a low key manner and then sent me the loveliest of reviews... together with an invitation to perform at the prestigious Malvern Girls School.

> Having already seen the television production 'Catherine', it was with great curiosity that I attended the premiere of Mark Wheeller's adaptation at the Oaklands Community School.
>
> The play begins and ends with an amusing version of Billy Goats Gruff, an interesting commentary on the pressures parents place on their young. It is perhaps difficult to appreciate how humour can play a part in such a tragic story but the cast manage to integrate it well. Music too plays a prominent role, particularly that of Karen Carpenter. 'Desperado' took on a new and powerful meaning within the context of the play.
>
> The production cleverly avoids having to present the gradual deterioration of Catherine. As she nears her death, her mother addresses the audience directly and we are shown slides of her daughter. They evoked gasps of horror from the audience. The technique of addressing the audience is used by both father and mother and as a result our sympathies lie with them as they do battle with an increasingly wilful offspring. Catherine makes no such direct contact. Her remoteness is further emphasised by the occasional regression into puppet-like movements.

> The play is powerful and the young performers were excellent. For those knowing nothing about anorexia they would at least come away aware that many complex issues are involved, and the dreadful finality if everything fails.

This reaction was so supportive of our efforts.

Next we were to hear the views of the press. First the locals... then, increasingly the nationals. What would they make of it?

The views of the press

Two local papers reviewed it. No one had any idea quite how important these words would prove to be, to me, the cast and indeed the plays future.

REVIEWS

Sue Wilkinson – Daily Echo

The best treatment Kylie Minogue – the Neighbours star allegedly suffering from anorexia nervosa, and those like her could have, is a front row seat at this play.

It will shock, disturb, educate and move with its innovative and imaginative telling of the true tragic tale of a girl who died from the condition.

Slides of the real Catherine, weighing three stone, brought gasps of horror and the scene of Abigail Penny, who plays Catherine, bingeing was genuinely disturbing.

Director Mark Wheeller and the marvellously energetic and talented ensemble have not judged or waved accusing fingers. This documentary like play is understanding of Catherine's suffering, indicates the inadequacy of hospital treatment and poignantly shows the family's torture.

An adaptation of the Billy Goats Gruff story acts as bookends to the play and aptly illustrates parental pressures on youngsters – a trigger of the syndrome – and the reluctance to relinquish childhood.

REVIEWS

Laurie Dorman – Southampton Advertiser

It was with compassion and commitment that the students of Oaklands Youth Theatre presented the moving story of Catherine Dunbar's struggle against anorexia nervosa. Edited by Oaklands Head of Drama, Mark Wheeller, the play highlights the causes and controversial treatment of the disease.

Abigail Penny took the lead and, watched by Catherine's mother, convincingly portrayed the skeletal young girl fighting something that she neither understood nor accepted. There were pitiful scenes of extreme bingeing and, as slides showing Catherine at three stone were displayed, a shocked silence blanketed the audience.

A most mature account, sensitively and enthusiastically performed. Bravo!

To my relief there were lines from these reviews we would be able to use in our Edinburgh hand-outs. Now, we had to hope for something as good from the Times Educational Supplement... a heavyweight national paper who taken time to come to our school theatre to review our work.

We had to wait. The TES came out weekly and reviews weren't included immediately.

My experience of TES reviews had been mixed. Hugh David, tended to leave early and then hammer the production. Just as I left Epping we had one fabulous review from Nick Baker for Too Much Punch For Judy. I asked if we could have Nick as our reviewer but now, I was living in the south of England. We had to have someone more local; Mick Martin.

I found out little about him other than he was a playwright too, based in nearby Salisbury. I was fearful he wouldn't take to the documentary approach. My (limited) experience was that it was not liked by many "proper" playwrights. When the review was finally printed, I couldn't wait until I had paid for it so stood in the shop transfixed. It was longer than the local reviews...

THEATRE REVIEW

Adapted from Maureen Dunbar's biography of her daughter, Catherine uses simple narrative and a series of stylised visual tableaux to build a powerful and often harrowing chronicle of Catherine Dunbar's long and ultimately unsuccessful, fight against anorexia nervosa.

The show is both uncompromising and sensitive in its examination of anorexia and its ability to raise our awareness of a condition about which we remain woefully ignorant defines it as an important piece of work. The power of Catherine, however, derives more, obviously from its documentary authenticity, and from the commitment of a talented young company than from its purely dramatic qualities and highly charged domestic tragedy.

For Mark Wheeller's script has an unfortunate tendency to fall into a sort of theatrical no-man's land somewhere between clinical case study (all facts, figures, weights and dates), and highly charged domestic tragedy.

The real problem is that the play falls short of giving genuine dramatic substance to the family trauma which it uses as its focus. The set-pieces are inventive and often effective but, they are used chiefly to provide unnecessary illustration of the narrative, rather than to elucidate the crucial emotional complexities which underlie it. We're left with too many unhelpfully one-dimensional characters, whose reactions are laconically explained rather than properly explored.

"I was torn in two." says Catherine's mother at one point. Well, quite... but surely, we shouldn't need to be told. That said, Wheeller's direction has a painful ebb and flow that captures, in general terms, the essence of the families ceaseless trek back and forth between hope and despair, compassion and frustration. And, there are mature, confident performances from the principal actors, led by Abigail Penny, with a well sustained, moving interpretation of the title role, which is particularly impressive in its avoidance of overstatement.

The enterprising company are taking the show to the Edinburgh fringe, where it should be compulsory viewing for anyone connected with the care or education of teenage girls.

Mick Martin

I was devastated. All I could see was the negative stuff about me as a writer from someone I deemed to be a "proper playwright". All our efforts to make it more than a "series of facts and figures" had, according to Mick, failed.

"One-dimensional characters" was something I'd been criticised for in previous documentary plays. Was this, once again, highlighting the limitations of my work or of the form? Would this review foreshadow its reception in Edinburgh with a more 'theatre literate' audience? We had no time to make alterations. We were stuck with a play that seemed destined to fail! Arghhhhhhhhh!

That was my initial reaction. This was not how I would sell this review to the cast. I needed to be positive... and keep things in perspective. The Drama Adviser, local papers and our own audiences had reacted favourably.

Promoting the play

It was very easy to extract a decent quote for the hand-out, focussing on the power of the performance and my direction. These quotes managed to make it seem as if the TES had really loved it. Haha! Soon I forgot that Mick hadn't been a total fan and, after another successful performance at the Fareham Arts Centre, we were off to Edinburgh for our official premiere with the TES quote adding to the hype!

Mmmm... the hype. I remember being aware of the rewards hype might bring. Any David Bowie fan knows this. His way of becoming famous was to behave as though he was. I openly admit I was doing everything I could to be "spotted" at the Fringe as I knew many others had been![10]

I remember cheekily inserting the phrase "highly acclaimed" with reference to my previous work in both the Fringe programme and our Edinburgh publicity handouts. I was aware this was stretching the truth but no-one ever questioned it or commented on it to me. Perhaps my "hype" provided the start to my being considered a "veteran"? I think, it's fair to say, even I began to believe it and was shocked that our audience numbers remained pretty low (between 6 and 36 if memory serves correctly) in a venue where we would have attracted many more, had my work actually have been "highly acclaimed".

We were performing from Monday 29th August until Saturday September 3rd at 3:45pm. Tickets were £2.50 with concessions £1.50 (equivalent to £6.50 and £3.50 in 2017).

> *Heading up to Edinburgh for the Fringe in 1988 gave us a genuine sense of what being 'in theatre' actually meant. Being in an entirely new show and waiting for our reviews in The Stage and spending the daytime finding ways to drum up audiences for our performances was both eye-opening and exhilarating!*

Chris Vaudin (Baby Goat & Double Yellow Line)

---

[10] Chris Vaudin (double yellow line) was "spotted" by one of Nigel Martin Smith's scouts and invited to audition for the group that eventually became Take That!

OAKLANDS YOUTH THEATRE

CATHERINE
Heriot Watt Downstairs (Tic Toc 2) August 29 to September 3
3.45pm Tickets £2.50-£1.50

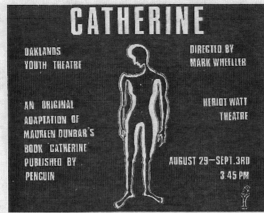

CATHERINE

OAKLANDS YOUTH THEATRE	DIRECTED BY MARK WHEELLER
AN ORIGINAL ADAPTATION OF MAUREEN DUNBAR'S BOOK "CATHERINE" PUBLISHED BY PENGUIN	HERIOT WATT THEATRE AUGUST 29—SEPT.3RD 3.45 PM

2nd January 1984: Catherine Dunbar dies after her seven year fight against Anorexia. How can it be possible that someone with so much to live for can succeed in literally starving herself to death? Originally a best selling book...An Award winning T.V. film...Now a new play devised by Mark Wheeller (Author of the highly acclaimed RACE TO BE SEEN and TOO MUCH PUNCH FOR JUDY) with the Oaklands Youth Theatre. Potentially a big success!

Tic Toc 2 _____ *Page 11*

We had no reviewers until the Wednesday performance, which was so disappointing. We heard that the all-important Scotsman review would be published at 2am in the morning. I clearly remember staying up and wandering out to get the review with another teacher and a couple of the older members of the cast from a news stand we knew was open for enthusiasts, like us, at this god-forsaken time. It was, I remember, quite a trek. We were well aware, as we read it, that everyone, back at our flats, was waiting for us to return. They were all so excited to see a glowing review from the Scotsman. What we read was about as glowing as a stage in a power-cut.

REVIEWS

Hayden Murphy – The Scotsman

This is a grim theatre musical. It is in the afternoon on a well-lit set in Heriot Watt Downstairs Theatre. It is an adaptation, by director Mark Wheeller, of Maureen Dunbar's book about Catherine. The cast is young and I'm a bit dubious about this concentrated hyper-activity being used as entertainment. Don't be misled by the Fringe brochure claim that this is a "newly devised" piece. It is not. It is a formula-Fringe show; biography, social commentary, dance routines and songs surround the death, in her early 20's of Catherine (Abigail Penny). She was the product of a divided home and a bewildered medical response.

Anorexia is known where appearance controls all appetites. The victim wastes to death because they feel their size and weight do not conform to an acceptable norm. It could be a loaded analogy for a valueless society. Unfortunately, in this format by this talented company it becomes a vehicle for another obsession, the director's vanity. I found the whole business, apart from personal despair for the central character, exploitative.

I had not re-read that in nearly 30 years until this moment of typing it out. It brings back how I felt on first reading it that night vividly! I had remembered the comment about the cast dancing around her death. That's all I remembered. I had completely forgotten how harshly it attacked me. I realise why I recall so clearly, the hype I conducted in the publicity. I remember thinking, my arrogant (false) claim in the Fringe programme had truly bitten me on the bum… hard!

I remember opening the door to our flat, a cheer going up from the whole cast as we arrived back Scotsman in hand but not held aloft. We tried to do everything to convey the tenor of the review. We failed. The cast were not having it. One photographed me with a very stern expression, as I entered the flat.

I remember saying to everyone the review was "terrible". No one believed us! They all thought we were winding them up. It was awful!

I think the accompanying teacher then read the review out loud to everyone, then they gradually realised we were not winding them up.

There was silence.

Finally... I think it was Debra who piped up.
"We still love you Mark!"

That made me feel a little better... though not "highly acclaimed"!

I'm not sure how to follow this. Life throws some curious curveballs. When we arrived at the venue that day, people were congratulating us. Unbeknown to us, on that same day, Friday 2nd September we had been listed in The Independent in their Daily Guide to the Best of the Fringe!!! How does that work? I imagine they must have reviewed us but we were unaware of it and to this day I have never seen that review.

We did the final two performances and, I'm delighted to report, we received a standing ovation from our final audience!

My final memory of Edinburgh that year, was ordering the biggest and most expensive Chinese takeaway I've ever ordered. At the end of it, Matt Allen, (visiting us from Epping Youth Theatre/Ape Theatre Company) did some fire-eating in our little front room! He was so close to us we could feel the heat of the flames coming out of his mouth. I don't think Health and Safety these days would cope but it remains a highlight of the Festival for me!

When I returned to School I discovered a letter from someone I didn't know. How kind that they had taken the time to write to me.

Dear Company,

I have just returned from a few days at the Edinburgh Festival where I saw 16 productions. Some were mediocre, some were good. Yours was excellent. Only after the curtain call did I remember that I was seeing a young people's production. I was going to leave a message of congratulation on your minibus but was still too moved to know what to write.

All the best for the new term and your future productions.

Terry Oakes, Barnes, London.

Edinburgh hadn't been the unmitigated success we had hoped for... but it had been an "experience"... and, I still maintain, a mostly positive one!

Dear Mark and Rachael,

Thank you so much for giving me the chance to take part in the play 'Catherine' and of course taking it to the Edinburgh Festival. I have had a tremendous time from start to finish.
I wish you every success with future productions. I only hope that I will be fortunate enough to be in league with such a "vain" director in the next "grim musical" you write!
Seriously though, I have had a great time right from the beginning of 'Race To Be Seen'.

Chris Vaudin x

Casting changes

Edinburgh proved to be the end of an era with the loss of our two oldest cast members. Deanne had been such an influential role model from the outset and then took on the responsibility of playing Maureen wonderfully. Andrew, had arrived late and taken on the role of John. He had been a key factor in keeping the ship sailing and found us exciting new avenues to explore in the way we presented the play.

We had gained much from their involvement. Losing these two older cast members could have destroyed us, but those that remained were now a year older, more mature, had shown proven commitment and were now significantly more experienced performers. The future looked bright... and I had further plans for the production which would mean re-casting these key roles. Debra (Giles) would make a perfect Maureen. Even though she was only 14 years old she seemed to have such qualities of caring and compassion in her real life that I felt certain she could use them in 'becoming' Maureen.

It's a very powerful thing at that age to be given something significant to do (and feel deep down you have an ability) – because, in the tricky teenage years, to feel you have something that's yours, and no-one else can take it away from you, is immense. I didn't ever think of ways to seem older. I didn't try to do the lines differently. Maureen's situation triggered off my own feelings.

Debbie Giles, looking back now, taken from a contemporary national newspaper interview by Vera Lustig.

John proved a more difficult problem. We had no older boys and Richard, who was by now 16, still looked too young. I wasn't sure what to do. Somehow, I was put into contact with Fawahd Ahmed, who was studying Drama locally and seemed willing to join us. He had an air of authority and a distinguished demeanour that matched the role (as I saw it) perfectly. Obviously, Fuzz (the name we came to know him by) was stepping into a role that was far removed from his own ethnic background. I decided this shouldn't be a consideration, in fact, he would possibly be able to draw on his own experiences of class and the role of men within his culture to play this role. I wondered if he would stay the course. Like Andrew, we took a chance... and it paid off.

Preparing for competitions

I was keen that, after all this work developing the play, we should enjoy opportunities that were open to us. The first was to enter the All England Theatre Festival, assuming we were able to reduce the play from a running time of about 75 minutes to under 55. We were determined to achieve this despite the fact that we weren't eligible, as a Youth Team, to qualify into the future rounds. I felt we could make an impression in the local (Totton) round and also, importantly, become part of the local theatre community.

Epping Youth Theatre had entered the AETF via the Waltham Abbey local round. I felt the competitive element could offer the cast us an additional motivation to improve. We had something 'different' to the kind of entries I had seen in Waltham Abbey and perhaps, as a consequence, we might do well... particularly as by now we had a much more experienced cast.

It would be relatively easy for us to get the performance further developed and ready by April, despite the cast changes and their various knock-on effects.

During the early part of the 1988/89 school year, a new national competition for Schools and Youth Theatres was announced. I decided to enter. It meant we had to show our performance to a National Theatre adjudicator in January. Our performance dates came forward a couple of months.

The Lloyds Bank National Theatre Challenge had, as it's prize, a performance at the Royal National Theatre (Olivier Stage) in July. I remember thinking 'that's rubbish!' I would have preferred a video camera for us to record our work in future!

Once again, we piled pressure on ourselves and were still keen to improve on what we presented at the Fringe. We were very much on a roll!

I had also had interest from Cambridge University Press (Act Now Series) to publish the play for schools but they had reservations about the title.

> ... It seems that plays which reveal something of themselves through their name sell better in the series than those titles that need a prior acquaintance with their content or theme. Whilst Catherine is clearly the subject of the play, it doesn't reveal anything about itself for the teacher/youth theatre director who does not know the piece ...

I was delighted with the alternative I came up with; Skeleton in the Pantry. It remains my favourite title for this play but was altered because I feared it may be considered insensitive.

It inspired the most incredible poster design by our own 14-year-old OYT member Chris Vaudin, who went on to design many other stunning OYT posters. Unfortunately, by the time Chris created this image, the title had changed once more; *Hard to Swallow*. It was never able to be used with the title that originally inspired it. The marriage of image and poster would have been perfect. Paul Harris went on to create the image that we used from that point on.

On the 12th January we showed our fresh new production, Skeleton in the Pantry, at the Institute of London to visiting schools. We were lucky enough to have some reviews from these students to mark this first performance with the 'new' cast.

From the very beginning of the performance, they captured the interest of the audience with an imaginative performance. Unlike the film, where you feel it was happening to someone else, you feel as if you are there with them, aching for it to stop.

I was surprised by how professionally the central characters and supporting cast took on various roles. They used many different drama techniques such as mime, freezes, symbolism, repetition of actions/phrases and direct address to show people's attitudes. Use of very haunting music to move us from scene to scene was excellent in creating different moods - tension, sympathy support etc.

The ensemble also represented symbols and other objects by skilful use of space and movement. They created a house, a refrigerator and a car to name but a few. Their simple actions were perfectly timed.

At one point Catherine's diary is read by four different actors simultaneously. The jumble of voices showed us Catherine's state of mind - confusion and obsession. This idea was also used in a scene where her mother and father return from a holiday to …

... discover her in a heap on the floor. She wails, helplessly, 'I'm sorry Daddy!'

The ensemble copy her whimpering, as she lays there sobbing and her distraught father kneels to comfort her. Maureen kneels in silent prayer.

Catherine was presented in dull clothing with a painted doll's face. At times, she walked with mechanical movements to haunting music which showed her as a puppet, controlled by the anorexia (or possessed by a 'devil inside her'). She showed despair and a childlike non-identity.

I wanted so hard to feel sorry for Catherine but everything she did kept me thinking how selfish she was. I wanted to scream at her to stop her tearing her family apart and when, near the end she said 'I did it for you Mummy.' I almost hated her for the cruelty of her own self-destruction. This only shows my ignorance of this disease but I was not the only one.

The play ends as it starts with the Billy Goats Gruff. I found it confusing at the start but at the end everything fell into place.

... The young goat represented Catherine who was trying to eat food and cross the bridge from being a child to become a woman. The evil troll was the anorexia, an inner voice that kept her from the food. Jo the goat was her friend who had met Catherine in hospital. When it was her turn to cross the bridge, she managed it and defeated the disease.

I left feeling empty inside. I felt a sense of relief for Catherine who had escaped her miserable life and hoped she had found peace somewhere else. I felt a sad frustration for the family. As the plays director told us:

'Skeleton in the Pantry' doesn't answer any questions... it serves to pose many more.'

Given the serious nature of the subject we were dealing with, it may be a surprise to hear that the group of us presenting these performances were a very upbeat group. I remember few arguments. We were able to pull together consistently to create the best theatre we could possibly manage given our limited previous experience. In terms of group work I would describe it as nigh on perfect.

When you are involved in a project that is so much more than the sum of its parts, there's really no inclination for the parts to start causing trouble for each other! OYT members weren't 'family', they often weren't 'friends'. We'd created another entity entirely, one with its own special modus operandi and relationships.

We were the people that came together to do 'this thing'. I trusted every single member of that group to 'deliver' unwaveringly.

The travels of this amazing project enabled us to experience some incredible 'chalk and cheese' moments. For example, we performed at The Malvern School for Girls, where, to a girl, everyone was the daughter of a diplomat, an international business person, or (of course) minor royalty!!!

Their dorm walls were full of photographs of absent family members. I was intrigued as to how the family Christmas snap could take precedence over the Bros posters that were plastered all over my bedroom walls at that time.

I lapped up the opportunity to converse with anyone outside of our usual 'teen' circle. The play and its content opened doors to us, intellectually (and theatrically) which was incredibly stimulating. I was an 'experience' sponge! The interest shown to us was a factor that helped us maintain a pleasant working status quo as a group.

Sarah Blackman (Ensemble cast)

I remember the performance at Malvern Girl's School. The audience were literally a step away from us as we performed. I felt as though in some way we were giving these children/young adults an opening to discuss their feelings. We were actually opening the flood gates to talk freely about a taboo, mental illness.

Donna Batt (Mummy Goat)

Our performance in front of the National Theatre assessor was set for Friday 20th January in our own Theatre. We were excited. We were confident. We were upbeat.

A bombshell… and more changes!

I had no inkling of the bombshell that would arrive in the form of a handwritten letter delivered personally by Abigail, our magnificent central performer, playing 'Catherine'.

17th January 1989

Dear Mark,

I am now finding my school work and 'Skeleton in the Pantry' too much. I have come to the stage where I have to choose between giving school my full efforts or my part, Catherine.

I am currently behind on English (Lang & Lit) and Humanities where I have also lost my folder!

I spend two evenings a week after school in Art to catch up. In science, I have many tests that require a lot of revision. Even though I have private lessons in French after school it is not up to scratch.

Most importantly, I received a bad result in my Maths mock exam. I need to spend more time on it.

When I agreed to continue to do the play this year I was under the impression it would involve a few evenings before the two performances at Oaklands. If we got through to the competition we would also go to London in July to perform.

The number of performances has since escalated. Eight in the next month at various venues and then more in April for the AETF.

I have worked hard during my time at school and it seems silly to jeopardise my college entry, due to Skeleton in the Pantry, as I have no plans to continue with Drama.

Teachers constantly nag me to hand in work that I haven't done. This is so difficult for everyone studying GCSE's with coursework but I also have the addition of this play to contend with.

I have found being involved very rewarding, a terrific experience and I learnt a lot. I want to thank you and Rachael for giving me a chance to play such a major part in it but I feel my future is more important.

I will do the performances at Oaklands (27/29 Jan) but then feel I must stop.

I would love to help the new 'Catherine' when she is chosen if you would like me to.

I am sorry to let you and the cast down but I feel it is time for me to stop.

Love Abigail xxx

I was saddened by this but knew I needed to act decisively for both our and Abigail's sake. Abigail needed a quick release so she could focus on her school work, which, particularly given her lofty ambitions (to be a barrister), was supremely important. She had given much to the production and deserved the best treatment from us.

We needed to sort ourselves out fast and have a new Catherine ready to perform for the National Theatre adjudicator. Telling the NT that we had to change the main role after they had seen the production seemed unthinkable. If we were successful, it could jeopardise our possible selection not to mention the 'rubbish' prize.

We had a potential 'Catherine' in our existing cast. Someone who had proved herself in every possible way. She would bring something new and exciting to the role. It would give her a real challenge, but I sensed she would be up for it. There were 10 days to prepare her for the role.

There were 10 days to re-cast all the ensemble roles the "new Catherine" had, up until now, played in the production. Ten days... ten evenings... and only a few were available for us to rehearse.

Four rehearsals! We had to do it.

I decided to ask Sarah (Blackman) if she would play Catherine. In many ways I saw it as a solution to another problem. Sarah was badly underused and deserved much more than the play was currently offering her.

Sarah would be our new Catherine... if she agreed.

I talked to Abigail and, that evening after school, the two of us (Abigail and I) visited Sarah's house to let her know the plan. I have no memory of this... but Sarah does!

Seeing as we were practically living in the theatre most of the time in the run up to performances, it must have been the one day of the week that we weren't there that my front door bell rang. On the doorstep, stood side by side were Mark and Abigail. Abigail was smiling in a genuinely warm and excited manner. (What altruism!) Mark handed me another copy of the script.

Abigail's script.

Catherine's lines were highlighted in it.

The conversation took all of 30 seconds and went something like this:
"Abigail is not able to continue with OYT. She has other things she needs to prioritise at the moment. You have ten days to learn Catherine's lines".

I'm not sure if I wasted much time with a response.

I really, really hope I said 'thank you'.

I closed the door, and the script didn't leave my hand for the next week!

Sarah Blackman ('Catherine' from 1989-90)

When I arrived home, I sat down to type (yes type!!!) a letter of thanks to Abigail.

Dear Abigail,

I am writing to thank you for the tremendous amount of work and commitment you have given to both CATHERINE and SKELETON IN THE PANTRY. I am very sad you have had to make this decision and realise how hard it must have been for you.
I remember clearly the day I approached you about playing Catherine and how excited I was following our initial conversation. You have lived up to and beyond my hopes and have, as far as I'm concerned, proved to be the perfect Catherine in terms of reliability and ability. The play could not have been given a better start. A very sincere thank-you.
It is rewarding for me to know that people appreciate my efforts on their behalf and you (in fact the whole cast) have always been extremely appreciative and have, by doing so, helped me to settle in what was, last year, a new job.
Sarah is, I'm sure, thrilled to have the opportunity of playing such a challenging role and will be very good. However, one of the key members of our cast will be missing and can never be replaced. It won't be the same. We will carry on and we will continue to enjoy our work, but we will constantly be reminded of you by so much of the play.
The door to OYT will always be wide open to you and I hope that you will choose to be involved in something we do in the not too distant future when the pressure is off. Even if you don't come back to OYT again, I hope you take on other acting parts at sixth form, college or university, or adult groups. You do enjoy it and I am sure that you have not exhausted your enthusiasm.
It is very difficult to write letters such as this. I can truthfully say that I have had a pretty continuous lump in the throat as I've been typing it, remembering many events of the past year. I can't say the words that I have chosen are the right ones but they are well meant.
I hope you make a determined effort to keep in touch with us all… even when you have left school.

Best Wishes,
Mark

We had ten days… only four rehearsals to prepare ourselves for our adjudication form the National Theatre. There were 375 entries. 13 performances would be selected. We had a 3.5% chance of being selected.

Four rehearsals!!!

I remember absolutely no panic about this cast change. Everyone, including Sarah, took it in their stride. It was as though it was meant to be.

We used those four rehearsals well. The independently commissioned reviews from our local papers came out as we awaited the NT adjudication.

REVIEWS

Sue Wilkinson – Southampton Daily Echo.

Skeleton in the Pantry

This is a revamped version of OYT's shocking and disturbing play, Catherine, based on the life of a girl who died of anorexia nervosa. It is shorter than its predecessor and has been polished for performance in front of a drama competition judge but it has lost none of its substance. The awful destruction caused by the eating disorder, the helplessness of victims' families and the lack of medical understanding have been more clearly defined.
Last minute cast changes meant Sarah Blackman replaced the original Catherine, Abigail Penny. She did wonderfully well.

Marc Morley – Southampton Advertiser

The anguish of Catherine and her family are starkly chronicled with graphic illustrations of her eating binges where she literally ate herself sick as well as times when she would take 100 laxatives a day.

Under the direction of Mark Wheeller this was a strong and convincing production with all the parts played well. OYT are made up of 13-19 year olds and they bring a good deal of enthusiasm, vitality and a great deal of professionalism. More group devised stories from the community are in the offering. They will be well worth watching.

It must have been an immensely pressured time for Sarah which, I think, I probably took for granted. I will take this opportunity to thank her for dealing with this so well. Amazing!

Feedback amongst the group had always been open, shared and direct. Part of our evolution as a group was in developing thick enough skin individually and collectively to deal with it. On one occasion Matt Allen (from Ape Theatre Co.) came to watch a performance which was one of my first as Catherine.

Matt was earning his theatrical chops and I saw him as a role-model, so his feedback was important to me. I still remember his response:

"In real life, Abigail is naturally more like Catherine."

'Oh no,' I thought, holding my breath, 'where's this going? He can't see past physical appearance or I've misjudged the whole thing?'

"But you, however, 'act' Catherine better".

I allowed myself to exhale.

I will forever be grateful to Matt for his diplomacy! As an actress in the making, I was over the moon he thought I had given a great performance even though I had nothing in common with Catherine as a person. He managed to praise my performance without detracting from Abigail's.

Once I inhabited that role I wanted to push Catherine to the edge. It wasn't the be all and end all for her. It was to me. I wanted my performance to be 'button pushing'. I didn't want people to have the option of hiding from it. I enjoyed their reaction and wanted their feathers ruffled. I was really grateful that Matt seemed to acknowledge that.

Sarah Blackman ('Catherine' from 1989-90)

Matt pretty much nailed it. Abigail had been perfect to start off with and almost "was" Catherine. Sarah brought a quality of "performance" to the role. It made quite a difference to the whole feel of the piece. It was never overplayed but there were more extremes in Sarah's portrayal. The binge was, for example, messier.

Playing Catherine and Approaching the Binge Scene

The binge scene always gave rise to questions from the audience.

"Are you genuinely swallowing all that food, it looks like you are?"

Followed by,
"How can you physically binge and digest it on stage?"

Yes I was really eating it, all of it. In direct contrast to some of the stylised scenes in the play this scene was to be as realistic as possible and conducted in 'real time'. There was never a discussion between Mark and I that we would use any 'smoke and mirror' effects, or theatrical devices to fake ingesting that amount of food in that manner. It was a given we'd do it for real.

I remember my first rehearsal of the scene. I laid out the food items in a way that felt 'comfortable ' to me which also let the audience see what was there; packets of cereals, yoghurt pots, chocolate bars, left-overs from last night's dinner, cold sausages, baked beans, packets of crisps and the centre piece - the Bird's custard trifle in a glass dish! At this first rehearsal, Mark probably said something really helpful like:

"Go!"

And so, I dutifully 'went!'

Other members of the cast were simultaneously reciting Catherine's diary entries and one ear was tuned to those for familiar pointers acting as signposts; a certain word here from Donna, a line there from Martin, a diary date from Gary, etc. If I'm not mistaken, the actors ended up having to shout a lot of the lines as they came to the end of the recitation to ensure I could actually hear them to start 'winding down'.

I was in charge of purchasing the food. I looked at the diary entries and using that as the limiter I collected types of foods which required different rhythms (speeds) to chew and be swallowed. For example:

Yoghurt: not much chewing was needed and it was easy to swallow.
Rice Krispies: a few chews were needed but these were easily helped down by the
                  yoghurt.
I played with those rhythms.

Externally the binge had to look like the ultimate spontaneous explosion of hitherto suppressed impulses. Although each binge was different, I was also 'conducting' the action like a musical conductor; slower here, (eat this), faster there, (so eat that), reach a crescendo, (mix that with this) now a diminuendo... a quick pause here for self-loathing and repulsion, a moment now for tears of anger etc.

Pace-wise I didn't see this scene as different from any other in the play, it still had to have 'dynamics'. I hoped this rhythmic element added to the realistic – and also dramatic nature of it.

When you see an interpretation of psychologically damaged people in a sanatorium, you invariably see people rocking, twitching, scratching at themselves, self-harming or fiddling with their hair. At first glance this can seem a bit like visual stereotyping, but, like many stereotypical actions, they are based in reality. 'Ticks' come to the fore, along with repetitive movements, and a sense of turning in on oneself, as if an almost 'animalistic' physical or biological rhythm is rising up from the subconscious of the person and taking over. I wanted to harness that aspect of animalism and demonstrate the visceral strength of the bingeing impulse reigning supreme over Catherine's mental effort to control them.

We had Catherine sitting on the floor for this scene, another way of highlighting this primal element was to sometimes rock gently backwards and forwards, as if in the throes of a rhythm she could not control, and conversely, she was also trying to nurse and placate herself at the same time.

Unsurprisingly I hadn't seen anyone in the throes of a binge. My interpretation came from this visceral instinct.

I think we only rehearsed the scene once, mainly for the sake of timing, and for Mark to see I'd got the gist of it and then 'that was that'.

It was the scene Mark gave the least feedback on, maybe because he was happy with it, or possibly because it felt a bit awkward or intrusive to watch? Possibly he felt uncomfortable that someone had to actually do it in the first place without artifice?!

We talked about the 'blessed trifle' and having to clean the mess of it up afterwards, but we never discussed any potential impact it might have had on me or anyone else in the cast. I think that's because I gave Mark all the right signals that everything was 'ok' in that department and it was business as usual, just like any other scene.

Our focus was on its impact on the audience, remember, in 1987, this kind of expose was revelatory stuff! We were lifting the veil on these hidden activities. The general public didn't know what anorexics did or what was going on behind closed doors.

This graphic portrayal, coupled with Catherine's personal outpourings during the scene, was a heady mix and confrontational for an audience at that time. There was no escape for them visually or aurally! It wasn't a scene left to audience interpretation or one you could tune out from, it was a stark, literal representation. From the feedback we received, it was enlightening and it hit some people like a sledgehammer.

Sarah Blackman (Catherine 1989-90)

The anger was wilder.[11]

Try standing opposite the most wonderfully warm hearted Debra O'Sullivan (nee Giles), knowing that in ten seconds you have to slap her... really slap her... hard in the face and see how you feel. It wasn't easy.

I don't know if our collective stage combat skills were so weak as a group that we tried to fake it but couldn't, or if we just weren't willing to run the risk of a dud hit not 'connecting' and undermining the scene, but it transpired that the hit would be a hit!!! My first attempt would probably have been hesitant, ridiculously unnatural and half aborted mid-air.

The second would have seen me trying to make the slap look hard but to keep it soft – which is practically impossible

The third was... well... a slap to the left cheek.

---

[11] You can see this slap (and the original binge) on the DVD of *Hard to Swallow* where extracts from a 1990 OYT performance in a hospital lecture theatre is a bonus feature. Available from Wheellerplays@gmail.com

> *I take my hat off to Debra for playing that scene as if she genuinely didn't know what was coming. Not once did she give any indication of it. I got to see her expression during the preceding dialogue and she never - I mean never - came out of character before I hit her, not for a second. Not a flinch, not even a flicker in the eyes that she was steeling herself for it.*
>
> *THIS was a gift to me and allowed me to do it 'in character' without creating the mental hurdle of 'hitting and hurting Debra.*

Sarah Blackman (Catherine – 1989-90)

And what did Debra make of having her lights punched out every performance by a close friend?

> *I think at that age you don't dwell and overthink things. I had to be slapped, and that was that. And it had to be authentic.*
>
> *I don't really recall Abigail slapping me, but I do Sarah, because a) we were good friends and had that connection which probably added an extra edge and b) she just went for it! This was a good thing. There were a couple of times it really smarted and my eyes watered - and that was equally a 'gift' as I had to deliver some quite powerful lines afterwards.*
>
> *Looking back, I feel huge empathy for those words now that poor Maureen had to convey.*

Debra Giles (Maureen 1989-90)

The comedy (which had always been Sarah's forte) brought a cheekiness and made Catherine more endearing. The sensitive moments seemed quieter because they played off the other extremes. It was fascinating seeing the whole performance alter with this one cast change.

For the sake of the journey of this play, this turn of events provided an unexpected stimulus and boost. The cast were incredibly focussed in those four important rehearsals. We were really up against it but we pulled together... not for the sake of the adjudicator but for Sarah and our own pride.

When it came to the 28th we were ready! We were excited rather than nervous!

Peter Rowlands, the editor of the Cambridge University Press was keen to push for publication within his series and was in the audience. In a letter to me afterwards, he highlighted how impressive Sarah had been:

> It was a very skilled piece of ensemble work, particularly with such a young cast. I envy you the process of working with them over the next few years and watching them consolidate and build on their skills.
>
> Invidiously, I have to mention the young girl who played Catherine whose confidence and sensitivity was utterly remarkable.

My longstanding friend (and former Stantonbury Youth Theatre member) also came to see it on the 28th January.

> Catherine's tragic story was dealt with in such a professional way by all concerned both on and off stage. My sympathies shifted from character to character. Emotions changed from sorrow, anger, frustration and guilt and kept me riveted. Some of the greatest playwrights of our time would have been really proud of this.
>
> Thanks for producing a piece of theatre that I shall always remember, think and talk about.
>
> I sincerely wish you every success in the Lloyds Bank National Theatre Challenge and the other competitions. You have a piece of Theatre that is most thought-provoking and the best I've seen in a long while. It so deserves full recognition. Well done!
>
> David Nurse

It's always tense watching the play with the real people in the audience. It certainly heightens the tension. Sarah's father had the experience of sitting next to Maureen at this performance.

> *During the scene where Catherine is forcibly sectioned, I would go 'hell for leather' physically and verbally in an effort to fight off everyone who is trying to restrict me. I found out later that, during this scene, my father must have reacted physically or flinched, because Maureen turned to him and whispered "now you know how I felt".*

Sarah Blackman (Catherine 1989-90)

71

Chapter 5

Drama Festivals and Competitions

I was far from optimistic about the Lloyds Bank National Theatre Challenge. The only thing I had ever won was a football trophy (for best footballer) when I was 12 years old.

So, despite thinking what we were doing was good, I thought we had little chance of being selected. The reviews from the two heavyweight papers offered some evidence for 'Theatre types' not really 'getting' what we were up to.

Had I known the background of our NT assessor, Tony Gouveia, I might have been more hopeful. Tony passed away earlier this year but David Johnson (Theatre Centre), wrote this about him in his obituary:

> *He (Tony) had been a huge success as an actor/singer in West End Musicals but I realised he was not dedicated to become a star. He was much more interested in supporting and facilitating young people in areas and places of need.*

I would have told the cast (repeatedly) how my (older and more experienced) Epping Youth Theatre entered the National Student Drama Festival the previous year. I had been so confident of them being selected (with their 'acclaimed' production of *Too Much Punch For Judy*) that I organised a party (and paid for much of the food!!!) on the day the results were announced. We weren't selected and the party was a complete washout. This remained fresh in my memory.

I hoped we would win but could not put my eggs in this basket. We had the back-up of having entered the local Drama Festival in Totton. I imagined making that the climax to this set of performances and then moving on to something new.

When Tony talked to us afterwards he seemed to like what we had done. I remember thinking the cast were fantastic and came across as passionate and unusually committed. I remember Tony being particularly impressed by the set-up we had at Oaklands, especially the support we had from our Head teacher, Peter Hollis. He really had vision for Drama at Oaklands and, as I often said at the time, put his money where his mouth is. It was wonderful that his support did not pass by unrecognised.

We had done the best we could. That was a relief. We waited for the formal assessment to arrive. It was nerve-wracking opening the envelope... something akin to receiving exam results.

The Performance
This 70-minute show follows the life of Catherine Dunbar through her suffering with anorexia to her death. The story was told through narration to the audience and by stylised images of what was being reported, such as the force-feeding in hospital. This quite simple technique was very effective in creating emotional tension which kept the audience riveted.
The ensemble work was superb as was the overall ability to communicate to the audience and with each other. Changes from episodes flowed, with robotic movements, crowd activities etc. and were disciplined. They demonstrated the result of a lot of hard work. Especially worth mentioning within this excellent cast were the performances of Debra Giles as the Mother and Sarah Blackman, who took on the role of Catherine with one weeks rehearsal.

The Script
Anorexia is a potential problem for a lot of young women and this script describes one person's experience graphically, sensitively and in language that communicates directly to an uninformed audience (and I suspect to potential victims of this condition). The style of the dialogue ranges from sharp one sentence statements to intimate conversation and descriptive monologues. It never feels contrived due to the excellent directing which keeps the style consistent. As a script for an ensemble it challenges everyone with lots to do and focus on.

Technical
Performed end on with two tables, a raised rostrum and slide screen. Costumes were consistent and great. Lighting was well used and creative. 17-year-old Kalwant Singh should be well proud of his work.

Music
Taped 'Carpenters' music was used to move the play from episode to episode. This was decided as a tribute to Karen Carpenter, who died of anorexia. I don't think the music integrates into the exposition of the play integrally.

The Group
Ages 14-18. This group came together to work on this piece, although some of them had worked together before. They are keen and very committed to this play which has gone through several changes with consistent loyalty.

Other Comments
This is a well devised and entertaining drama documentary which informs brutally and sensitively. I would like to see it performed in schools and backed up by an educational workshop and support material. Maureen Dunbar, whose book about her daughter provided the plot for this show was in the audience but this did not visibly unnerve the cast who really went for it!

We were soon told we had reached the final 200. We had more visits from more assessors in other performances but had no idea when we would hear the final selection news.

Meanwhile, we prepared ourselves (still developing the play/performance) for our first appearance at the Totton Drama Festival (part of the All England Theatre Festival).

On the morning of the 6th April, (our Totton performance date) I received news from the National Theatre.

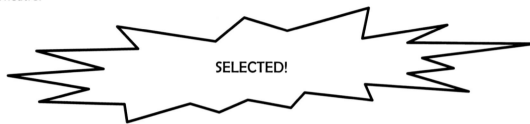

SELECTED!

Suddenly, performing at the Royal National Theatre was the best prize ever! I was so glad it wasn't "just a video camera"!!!

It was wonderful to arrive at Totton knowing we had achieved this national success. We were on top of the world!

Not only this... but the Catherine Dunbar Trust awarded us £4000 (£10k in 2017 terms) to help us to take the play further afield. We decided we would like to take the play to America.

We needed to fund raise a further £10,000 (£25k) to make this dream come true!

We formed a fund-raising committee (of mostly parents) who were incredibly proactive. We organised:

- Skittles Evening
- Quiz Nights
- 'Dining in style' evening
- OYT comedy evenings (June and November - as if we weren't busy enough preparing for the NT performance!)
- Jumble and Car Boot sales
- Individual sponsored events
- Christmas cards

These raised both awareness and a huge amount of money. We were on our way ... self-helping to the max ... and enjoying it a lot!

Inspired by Tony's comment in the NT Assessment I started to work with the newly formed StopWatch Theatre in Education Company to develop a professional tour of what I had by now decided should be called *Hard To Swallow*.

At Totton, four of the cast gained nominations for *Best Performer*.

We also won the *Best Youth Performance*!

The play was well interpreted by a Director and company whose commitment to the play was total. It was a quite outstanding example of teamwork.

Movement was particularly attractive. The ensemble work during the Billy Goats allegory, the 'Brussels sprouts' episode, and the hospital feeding routines all achieved effectively with great economy.

Catherine: A performance of great sincerity. Commendable vocal work ranging from hysterics to quiet reflection and a growing physical weakness.

Maureen: Conveyed the hurt, bewilderment, guilt and love. She had great vocal clarity, a quality of stillness with sincerity and considerable technique in her longer speeches.

John: A most unselfish performance conveying the anger and incomprehension well. His last speech was totally sincere, technically well delivered and extremely moving – one of the highlights of the play.

Other Cast: Their contribution to the performance was of equal calibre to the named characters. Patricia's final speech was full of suppressed emotion and very well controlled. A fitting climax to the play.

You had lavished upon this production care, attention and affection which resulted in a powerful and thought-provoking piece of theatre.

David Vince. GODA

I know there was heated discussion from the Festival organisers as, on the basis of our points score, OYT should have progressed to the next round.

> The AETF and other first round festivals were not letting youth groups go forward in the competition. They wanted youth groups to have their own trophy at the round one festivals and then go home even if they scored higher than adult teams.
>
> Being very enthusiastic about youth theatre and fair play, we pushed very hard for the highest scoring groups to go forward whether adult or youth. Eventually they listened and OYT deserved their place at the British Final in Scotland (with *'One Million to STOP THE TRAFFIK'*) in 2010.
>
> **Christine Farleigh – Chair –Totton Drama Festival**

We didn't mind to be honest! We had been selected to perform at the National Theatre!!! (I thought I'd mention it again to highlight our utter surprise and excitement!) We (felt we) were big news!

We had an incredible half page feature in The Independent! It is lovely to read of Maureen's reaction to the play.

> You'd think you couldn't possibly relate to a play about your own family performed by such young people, and yet, every time I see it, I'm terribly moved. I've seen it grow and develop and get better and better.

Vera Lustig had access to one of our rehearsals and it's pleasing to me to read her observations.

> Some teachers use a special voice when addressing young people – but there is no condescension in Mark's manner. In the long and intensive rehearsal, I watched, he was laconic in both praise and reproof, but afterwards he spoke to me warmly about individual cast members. Treating his performers as adults, and ensuring they participate in decision making, pays dividends in performance.

The Times Educational Supplement did a whole page feature about OYT and The Sunday Times featured us in their Sunday Colour Supplement! We felt we were the talk of Southampton (I don't think we were!)

A few days before the performance I had a phone call from Donna Batt's parents.

> Donna has broken her ankle. She's in plaster. I don't think she'll be able to perform. She's devastated.

I thought of Graham Salmon (Graham – Word's Fastest Blind Runner), his appeals for inclusion and his ability to dismiss or overcome obstacles. Here was my opportunity to decide something positive for Donna, who really deserved a bit of support in this moment of need.

> Of-course she can! She's a key part of this production. She needs to be on stage... even if she's in a wheelchair.

In the event Donna performed (wonderfully) in a wheelchair!

The National Theatre performance

I spent the whole day on 12th July 1989 at the National Theatre preparing for our performance that evening on the world-famous Olivier stage. Many of our friends and relations were there to support us. Not only that, but friends and relations of (Catherine and) Maureen Dunbar. It was incredibly exciting and I felt more important than I'd ever felt before... certainly more important than a man with a brand new camcorder!

During the technical rehearsal, I remember trying to stop the rehearsal. No one could hear me so I bellowed at the top of my voice. Everything stopped. Everyone looked at me. I checked myself... here I was... little Mark Wheeller... and everyone in the National Theatre had stopped because I wanted them to. I had arrived. Perhaps now I was 'highly acclaimed'!

I can't remember any of this performance (I do remember the announcement about Lord Olivier's death) other than Donna performing in a wheelchair as if nothing was wrong. I do remember sitting in the (huge) audience and feeling so, so proud of my young cast performing to this grand audience.

It was certainly a leap to go from our school theatre, to sitting next to Simon Russell Beale and his cast as they chatted over breakfast in the NT restaurant.

I'd seen a few shows at the National and had harboured a personal ambition to perform on its stages, so the competition being housed there was particularly poignant for me. I remember the Artistic Director shouting down some technical instruction to me from the auditorium during our tech rehearsal, probably something like 'Good-God woman! Stop! You're about to walk off the edge of the stage!' ... but in my head I thought, 'Oh my goodness, cherish this. You've just been 'directed' by Richard Eyre!'

The National was the one performance I didn't feel in control of. Not remotely. It was an out of body experience to be honest. I was expecting utter cognisance and the most finely tuned performance of my life, instead I got 'fighting blind' in a parallel universe!

Surreal isn't strong enough a word for it! Suddenly, a play I knew inside out felt completely alien to me, like it was being performed in a different language... and backwards!

The experience of a lifetime had somehow transmogrified into the stuff of nightmares. The performance itself was an adrenaline-fuelled blur. I assume, if I had spent the entirety of it facing the back wall or speaking in tongues someone would have told me by now, but I don't remember a second of it, apart from one walk across the stage to Catherine's desk which, historically, had taken a maximum of six seconds. On the Olivier stage it seemed to take a full six minutes... and in silence!

At one point, I thought I had gone deaf. I was stood in the wings waiting for my first entrance and started to panic about being able to hear my cue. The stage was so much larger than any we'd previously performed on. I couldn't hear people's lines, just the odd word now and again. I remember thinking the atmospheric pressure in that auditorium must be skewed because I felt physically oppressed.

Sarah Blackman (Catherine 1989-90)

I thought we'd made the big time when we performed at The National Theatre. There we were, a group of kids from Southampton, having vocal training by a professional on the Laurence Olivier Stage. I felt like I was an actor. At show-time I was standing back stage and Dr Who aka Sylvester McCoy stood next to me and gave me words of encouragement ... not an everyday occurrence!

Richard Brown (Simon)

We were amazingly proud to win the opportunity to perform on the Olivier stage at the National Theatre in 1989, even if the power of the play's message was somewhat undermined by the then Dr Who, hosting the evenings event, throwing chocolates (from one of the play's most emotionally charged scenes) out into the audience panto-style at the end!

Chris Vaudin (Baby/Double Yellow Line)

I remember meeting Catherine's brother and sister after the performance along with Tony Key, one of my Theatre mentors from the Lewisham based 4R Movement and Dance Group. It was so nice of him to come and see how I had used his inspiration. Sadly, that was the last time I saw him. He passed away a few years later. Tony had been a Goldsmiths' College tutor of mine who nurtured my enthusiasm and gave me endles opportunities to explore my creativity in his wonderful Community Theatre group. I miss him and owe him and his wonderfully bohemian lifestyle so much.

Maureen's literary agent was also in the audience. We met briefly and she said how impressed she had been by the play. Meg Davis took me on and I have been with MBA Literary Agency ever since. Also in that audience, unbeknown to me, was Ginny Spooner, who went on to be Edexcel's Chief Examiner in Drama. My work was promoted to teachers by Edexcel in a way I could never have dreamed of thanks, I believe, to that one performance.

That single performance went on to have a significant impact on my own future. More reviews came in from "posh" newspapers as a result of the NT performance:

THEATRE REVIEW

Hard to Swallow ... an instructive and disturbing cautionary tale ... but it did stray, occasionally into bathos.

Kate Kellaway - Observer

THEATRE REVIEW

The Billy Goats Gruff scene superbly illustrated the anorexic's reluctance to face the "trolls" of adulthood... Skilfully and movingly played.

Ann McFerran – Times Educational Supplement

There was also the review in the Stage and Television Today by Ann McFerran, (again) who went on to say.

THEATRE REVIEW

There wasn't a dry eye in the audience. Finely acted by the cast led by Sarah Blackman's first-rate Catherine, Hard to Swallow is a splendid testimony to this talented young company whose average age is 15, that of Catherine when she first became anorexic.

Ann McFerran – Stage and Television Today

OYT performing Hard to Swallow at the National Theatre on July the 12th remains the professional highlight of my career. It is all the more impressive that the cast were all so young and inexperienced. I remember thinking; they have not had to suffer any failure as they were selected on their first attempt to achieve something so prestigious. I think that will be good for them ... but perhaps they won't value it. Looking at what they have written (above) I had nothing to worry about.

Chapter 6

Climatic OYT HTS Finale

I consider what happened next to represent the apex of our very own holy (theatrical) trinity:

First the Edinburgh Fringe Festival (Fringe), then the performance at the National Theatre...
... then to top it all...
... a trip to Texas! Yee hah!

Mark might as well have taken us on a tour of Mars! So alien did our contemporaries' lives seem to me then. I remember being flabbergasted by the cultural differences between two nations who spoke the same language.

We were all paired with students from The Houston School for Visual and Performing Arts, which served as our HQ. I assume every student automatically graduates with a Masters in 'dancing on the tables at lunchtime'. Everyone, and I mean everyone, was up on the nearest available surface 'bustin' moves'! It was like 'Fame'... in cowboy boots!

We participated in some of their classes which was nerve wracking! I remember one exercise where we each had to share something we were 'afraid of'. Well, we Brits thought we'd done well by spitting out things you might expect such as 'dying', 'being alone' etc. and then one American student said;

'I'm afraid I'm going to take my dad's shotgun one of these days and kill him!"

I don't think anyone managed to top that one!

Guns, it turned out, were everywhere ... including, at one school we visited, the school canteen! A change from our British dinner ladies! It was wonderfully, bizarre.

The shared enthusiasm towards theatre proved the main bonding mechanism. One friend I still have, flew to the UK and we went to the Edinburgh Festival together.

We performed in many schools and colleges over the three weeks we were there. The audiences were very receptive to our performances. They really took things to heart. The Arts students took acting very seriously. They were very interested in how we could perform something like 'Hard to Swallow' and not be negatively psychologically affected ourselves.

We performed at a hospital during the Doctors' lunchtime. They brought their sandwiches with them to the auditorium and I remember thinking "this will be interesting when it comes to the binge scene..."

I found our American cousins much more open about their feelings than we were but with an incredibly earnest overlay. Our cultural overlay is dry humour. I'd sign up for the time-machine and relive these experiences again without reservation.

They were like inserting glorious technicolor onto our black and white seeming lives. It was manna from heaven for a teenager seeking heightened experiences. I don't think I slept much, there was always something to do, see, or someone to talk theatre-shop or personal ambitions with.

Sarah Blackman (Catherine – 1989-90)

It wasn't only the Youth Theatre members who felt like this was a trip to Mars. I did too. It was 1990. I was 32 years old. I had only been abroad four times in my life. Twice to France, on a school exchange and once (Christmas 1988) to Austria for my Honeymoon with Rachael. We also took our 3-month-old son, Ollie. We stayed with one of the teachers from the school.

We had spent this final year making a few minor alterations to HTS but mostly raising money for the trip including mounting a production of Too Much Punch For Judy which Deanne (previous Maureen) returned to direct and I assisted her with this. This gave cast who didn't have a main role in HTS an opportunity to do more. The cast, by this time were pretty seasoned performers and we showed both productions in and around Houston throughout the three weeks we spent there.

The link with Houston had been made by Hampshire LEA and the Central Bureau as a result of their involvement in the Teaching in the City Conference in New York.

I had not been involved in any direct conversations with the Houston School For Visual and Performing Arts (HSPVA) but was sent on a planning trip in May 1990.

I arrived in the Theatre of HSVPA to discover the Head of Theatre knew nothing about who I was or why I was there. No one else did either!!! I had travelled all that way and no one at HSPVA was expecting me. It looked like a disaster… but no, after showing him a letter confirming I wasn't a chancer, Bob Singleton (Head of Theatre Department) assured me that he would organise the visit. He was as good as his word. By the time I left, a few days later, he had organised homestay placements for all of our team! It was so willing and utterly remarkable!

In August 1990, we set off for Houston and soon encountered a 'bit of a problem'. At our Check-in, we were greeted by the police. A cast member was discovered to have a bladed knuckle-duster in his bag! He calmly said it must have been there from when his brother had borrowed his bag for camping. I couldn't believe it. I was convinced we were all going to be turned back. Fortunately, I had asked Pete Moody, the smoothest talking teacher (PE) I have ever known, to accompany us on the trip. We knew this secret communications weapon of ours was our only hope! Rachael moved me away and we left Pete to it! Remarkably, everyone at the desk accepted his well-chosen words. I viewed this as nothing short of a miracle. The bladed-knuckleduster was quietly confiscated and the cast-member was told that he would have to see how the authorities would deal with this on his return… and off we went!!!

I was so relieved we didn't have another cast change to make. It was quite a significant one… he was playing John!!!

> *From the moment we stepped on the plane, it hit me that we were actually going to America. I had never flown before. It was amazing but a weird feeling being up amongst the clouds! I was nervous though. After ten hours, we landed in Houston. My first view of the city was not what I expected. Everything is very spaced out and the roads are endless. I expected more skyscrapers.*

Taken from the Cast Diaries

We were hit by a shield of heat (102) as we left Houston airport. I remember all of us repeatedly going in and out to experience the heat shield. When we got into our various cars, taking us to our hosts houses, it didn't seem hot at all. It was, of course, our first experience of air conditioning!

We were greeted at HSPVA the following morning by two boxes of doughnuts (we really were in America!) and shared experiences of the students homes we'd been sent to stay in. Most had swimming pools and most had been (legally) driven to school by their 16-year-old student host. Sarah was ill and Debra stayed behind to look after her. That was a worry. Maureen and Catherine both unwell. I hoped they'd get rid of whatever it was fast!

The rest of the cast were thrown in at the deep end, after participating in a Voice Workshop (we never did warm-ups or voice workshops so, once again, it was like being in an alien environment). I was asked to show them the kind of (more improvised) approach to theatre we had. I asked our cast to demonstrate some short spontaneous comedy improvisation games which went down well!

We were all amused by the use of language (e.g. 'garbage') and we spent our first day 'orientating' ourselves. By the way I haven't suddenly recovered my memory but have discovered for these 21 days I kept a diary, as did all the cast.

> *The students are really friendly and everyone wanted to hear an English accent (We don't have an accent!) We rehearsed for the whole of the first day but never managed a complete run through! HSPVA students were interested in our plays today, rather than just us, so that is encouraging.*

Taken from the Cast Diaries

Kalwant had to acustomise himself to some high-tech lighting equipment. Meanwhile, we spent time re-devising the staging of the suicide scene. The work we did that day was to make the scene more physical by introducing body scenery to halt what I viewed as a dip in the play. I began, for the first time, to detect a slight reticence in the cast to keep on making changes. This could of course have been jet-lag, but it was something that had not cropped up previously!

Robert, the School's technician was a godsend. He had set up all the lights prior to our arrival and was keen for it to be exactly as we wanted. Nothing was too much trouble. I was impressed that this "magnet" school had attracted such committed teachers.

On Day 3 Sarah and Debra returned but Gary was ill and we were due to do our first two performances! Somehow the cast compensated for this and both performances were received by standing ovations from HSPVA audiences who really were theatre savvy. This was an impressive start! We went on to do an evening performance and we noticed the Americans were more open in their responses... there was more clapping and more crying!

We were very aware that this was a specialist school and wondered what these Arts specialist performers would make of our performances from a standard comprehensive school Youth Theatre group. It wasn't until this week that I really received a definitive answer. Following a request on Facebook for the US students to offer reactions to the play, if indeed they remembered it, I had these messages:

> *For a young Texan just hearing a British person speak was magical. From what I remember I was blown away that y'all would have tackled a subject so "deep" back then. It was a wonderful production and inspired many of us to find more of our own voices through work that was so thought provoking and new to us.*

Josh Jordan (HSPVA student 1990)

Wade Williams (HSPVA student 1990)

These comments came as a real boost when I saw them. I'd always felt we had made a good impression, but for them to remember it so vividly all these years later is a further testament to the quality of our youth theatre performers. We were only in HSPVA for a week or two!

Just to stress her commitment to our project, Maureen came with a friend to one of our performances. We did all we could to thank her for giving us all these various opportunities but it's nigh on impossible to express heartfelt thanks over and over again. Maureen had given so much of herself to us and we hoped she had gained something in return.

We participated in question and answer sessions, when requested, after some of the 16 performances we did over the three weeks. Schools were fascinated to come across anything like it... or us!

The Houston Independent Schools District provided us with a driver and an air-conditioned bus. We felt a bit overawed by their, and the host families', generous hospitality. An example of this, on a personal level, was that Rachael, Ollie and I were taken on an all-expenses paid trip to Galveston for the whole of the bank holiday weekend. Donna (one of the cast members) was taken to the New Orleans Jazz Festival by her family! Incredible.

Mark, Rachael & Ollie Wheeller at home with their host family the Rundsteins.

Richard Brown (Simon)

It was particularly gratifying for a performance to be given by 16-19 year olds to audiences of students and experienced doctors, many of whom were moved to tears.

Peter Vance (Deputy Head; Oaklands Community School)
From the formal Review of Houston trip.

Nothing is perfect and I will tell this story as it ended... not with any explosive climax but with a 'real' ending... warts and all. Debra hinted at it in what she remembered when I asked her, a few weeks ago, to send me her memories.

> *Looking back at the Houston experience, I can see the dream was starting to come to an end. All our lovely teenagerdom was almost over and we were breaking off. Nothing ever felt quite the same. It was all very intense and wonderful – we probably needed to go off and decompress and start to 'find ourselves' as young adults.*

Debra Giles (Maureen 1989-90)

My diary entries written during our visit to Houston round off the story... they tell of a teacher realising you can't always control everything... and for a teacher, it's very hard to let go!

Diary
Day 9

Sarah got herself involved in a controversial incident... driving a car without a license and without the owner's consent. Yesterday she was very 'light' about it and I felt, it needed to be dealt with. Ray (from HSPVA) agreed and joined (smooth-talking, miracle-worker) Pete and I to talk to her. She has assured me she will be "Little Miss Perfect"! Hopefully this is our glitch. Debbie seems to have taken umbrage by the way we spoke to Sarah.

Having said this, everyone went to Baylor College and did their best to do good performances with no time for a sound check.

Diary

Day 10

The final lesson today one of our students went awol. I over-reacted, partly because of yesterday. The atmosphere was not pleasant. I feel down about it and feel I've lost credibility as much as anything else.

Day 11

Deanne, and then I, did brilliant workshops, which helped bring the group together again, and helped me regain my confidence.

Day 16

Today I became resigned to the fact that important members of our group have lost their enthusiasm for the performance side. This is frustrating and disappointing but I do understand it.

Some have made the decision to leave OYT. Some have grown away from OYT and want out. They need to move on. The problem is that we still have to do the play. Although this minority are moaning, they all continue to turn in performances to be very proud of. I don't think I have ever had a group who can be so consistently inventive. The performance in the evening, although moaned about, was outstanding!

Diary

Day 17

Some performances have been done in the most difficult of circumstances... today we had a PA system giving out announcements during the performance and a noisy PE lesson in the next room! The cast were outstanding! I want the trip to be over. I am playing 'resigned', and am now treating a minority with kid gloves. Some are trying to be independent of the group.

Days 19 & 20

An excellent weekend. Everyone was relieved to have time off and we were relaxed and friendly. In the evening, we went to a surprisingly good comedy club. Lots of laughter.

We went to our final sun soak to Galveston. There are little frictions between group members but they seem to be undercurrents rather than wars. I am trying to take on a passive role to all of this, hoping that the adrenalin of the last few days will carry us through peaceably.

Diary

Day 21

We had a final reception. I made a speech and I was pleased to be able to thank the cast publicly. I hope they took in what I said because I have complete admiration of their skills and commitment.

We were thanked by the HISD for being such 'good and creative guests'.

We truly had an unforgettable time.

The final performances bought tears to our eyes.

Our last ever performance of Hard to Swallow was at Texas University Medical School. I thought it was going to be awful but the venue was lovely... a small arts centre, and the audience were brilliant. I got quite emotional at the end which I wasn't expecting. Everyone gave it their all. The audience praised our work highly and took the time to say so.

On our last evening in Houston, we had a barbeque for all the host families. It was a perfect atmosphere. It was a perfect way to end an exceptional trip. Youth Theatre (as we know it) is well and truly over. I shall miss the group. It's taken up probably the best part of my life so far and I'm just glad that I've been lucky enough to be involved in it.

Chapter 7

Professional Tour

By Adrian New (StopWatch Theatre Company)

Background

The story of the first professional production of *Hard to Swallow* contains as much coincidence and fortuitous meeting of people as does the story of its original creation as told by Mark in the rest of this book.

StopWatch Theatre Company was founded by Steven Pearce and myself Adrian New. We had been school friends, had gone off to different universities, kept in touch and decided that upon graduation in 1990, that we would start a theatre company together, in lieu of the year out so many of our peers had taken.

Adrian New (left) and Steven Pearce (left) Stopwatch Theatre Company Founders 1990

We were 21 years old and armed only with our degrees in English with Drama, and Performing Arts Management respectively to help us start a business and get our first show on the road.

A university project had brought Steven into contact with Mark. That meeting led Mark to invite Steven to use Oaklands School as a base for the company, in return for free workshops and performances for the school. This was a perfect win/win deal that enabled us to get on our feet and create and sell our first show. But what should that show be? Mark casually mentioned that he had recently written a play called *Hard to Swallow*...

We advertised for 4 actors and sent letters to about 300 schools across the UK. About 300 actors sent in their CVs and just 4 schools wrote back. Recruitment and booking a tour were both bigger challenges than we had anticipated. Our intention was to rehearse from mid-August to mid-September and tour thereafter. At the start of the summer holidays we did have our cast, but only a handful of bookings from October onwards. This gap was fortunate as our inexperience led us to casting some really unsuitable people who didn't like the script or our ideas for performing it. At the end of the first week of rehearsal there was mutiny and 2 of the 4 said they wouldn't be coming back.

Back to the drawing board. Rehearsals on hold. New auditions organised. This time we ended up with a team we could work with. Joanne Corser, Annette Joyce, Kate Pendry and Roland Taylor, with Steven completing the cast as well as directing and me taking on stage management and administration duties.

The Setting for the Professional Production

Touring to schools is more challenging than theatres as you simply don't know what facilities each space will have, or be without. Our set had to be flexible enough to work in drama studios, theatres and school halls. We also wanted to keep the audience close to us so settled on a ¾ round or thrust staging.

Theatre-in-Education has a duty to clearly communicate a message to an audience with more certainty than a purely theatrical performance. A theatre booker will want to know what a play is about. A school will ask "and what will they learn?" When telling a true story, a well-placed photograph in the performance is a stark reminder that this actually happened and could easily happen again. So we wanted to be able to project the slides of Catherine that Maureen had provided for Mark's production.

We borrowed from a local theatre 5 white flats that hinged together. This was our projection surface and our back drop that gave us a back-stage area behind. If the space was particularly tight, we could leave out a panel or two. In front of this we placed a table and chairs that were moved downstage into the thrust for key scenes. We also had a Kodak slide projector (35mm slides – this was long before the days of Powerpoint) with wired remote and a cassette player for our underscore.

Musical Underscore

One of the happy coincidences of our casting was that Roland was a gifted pianist and composer as well as actor. During the rehearsal process he wrote a number of pieces of piano music to underscore some scenes and to cover scene changes and transitions. These were recorded to cassette and played on a simple portable player. The subtle use of original music gave a wonderful texture to the performance. Unfortunately, those cassettes are long lost and so none of that music exists today.

Directorial "Decisions"

From the company only Steven Pearce had seen the OYT production. Without experience of the 'Wheellerplay' style, imagining how the more stylised sections should be performed was quite a challenge for the cast, and an even bigger challenge for Steven to direct them into effective performance. Our youth and inexperience did not equip us to win the battle with the cast to perform the play as written, so as rehearsals progressed, changes began to be made driven more by the confidence of the cast than the vision of the director.

As I look over my marked-up script now (nearly 27 years after the rehearsal process) I see that some of the most significant casualties are the more stylised elements that you might say are quintessential 'Wheellerplay'. I'm sorry to say that Jo the Goat did not make it into our production, and there are chunks of script which I would now view as essential to bring pace and a little light into this dark story with lines drawn right through them. We bowed to pressure to simply remove those sequences leaving us with a more straightforward naturalistic script with a mixture of monologue and acted scenes.

There was an even more controversial decision to include an argument scene between John and Catherine which was inspired by a similar scene included in the film of the story, but not present in Mark's script. The actors were adamant that to see John's frustration at his daughter's refusal to eat was key to understanding her motivation and so such a scene was improvised and included in our production.

In Retrospect…

If we were to undertake to produce the play now, our approach would be entirely different with a much greater understanding of the efficacy of Mark's style for young audiences and the ability to inspire actors to embrace that style. The review in the Times Educational Supplement described our production as "unsophisticated, but direct and intense" and I think this is a very fair assessment of the tone of our production. We focused on the narrative and missed the opportunity to enliven it with the stylisation opportunities that were presented to us but that we cut.

There is no video and no production photographs of StopWatch Theatre Company's first ever production. We gave 25 performances reaching from our Southampton base, east to Margate, north to Blackpool and west to Bristol. Feedback was good from the performances and a positive review in the Times Educational Supplement encouraged us to consider a second production for the Spring Term 1991. Our good and bad experiences in mounting this production were learnt from and 27 years on we continue to tour to schools across the UK. Having performed Chicken! over 5000 times, Arson About over 1000, and now enjoying huge success with I Love You Mum, I Promise I Won't Die, we have got much better at producing 'Wheellerplays', but this is the story of how it all began for StopWatch Theatre Company.

Chapter 8

Scheme of Work

The *Hard to Swallow – Easy to Digest* scheme of work is written to cover all the required learning for component 3 (Section A) Interpreting Theatre of Eduqas GCSE (9-1) Drama. It can also be adapted by teachers of other exam boards to use for the text performance assessment, where students perform two extracts from one play for a visiting examiner.

Teachers should check the copies they use are the correct version. The ISBN of the prescribed edition of *Hard To Swallow* is stated in the specification. Clean copies of the text may be taken into the exam. Teachers may decide to buy an 'exam copy' of the text which is not given to the students prior to their exam day, or they must advise students they cannot write in the text during lessons if those scripts are to be taken into the exam.

A student workbook is also available to accompany this book[12]. This contains a selection of worksheets and exercises that students can complete whilst studying the play following this scheme of work. Once completed, this can be used to revise the text in preparation for the written exam.

This scheme of work is designed to be run over a minimum of 5 weeks and the lessons can be adapted to suit your own timetabling requirements. The lessons run at 45 minutes of activity time, but are designed to be taught in an hour timetabled lesson time. This accommodates starting and ending the lesson and a warm up activity of the teacher or students' choice which is not included in the lesson plans.

Home learning activities have been included where appropriate. These can be incorporated into lessons to extend the scheme of work, and some lessons can be completed as home learning if required. Some lessons recommend pre-lesson activities, which may be incorporated into lesson time, depending on your schools homework policy.

There is no specific preparation required before starting the scheme of work. It is recommended that students prepare a performance at the end of the scheme of work which will give them a deeper understanding of the play. This task is started in lesson 16. Different groups could prepare

---

[12] This is available at www.karenlatto.com.

a section each, or the group can prepare a performance of the whole play. This will depend on the size and ability of the class. The performances can also be assessed as a mock text performance assessment for all exam boards which is externally assessed by a visiting examiner.

Scheme of work overview

Lesson	Specification content	Lesson focus
1	How the text is constructed and how performances create meaning through the characteristics of the performance text, including genre. How meaning is interpreted and communicated through performance conventions.	What is documentary theatre?
2	How the text is constructed.	Read through of the play with discussion
3	How the text is constructed.	Read through of the play with discussion
4	The social, historical and cultural context including the theatrical conventions of the period in which the performance text was created.	Who is Mark Wheeller? What is youth theatre? What is anorexia?
5	How the text is constructed and how performances create meaning through the characteristics of the performance text, including structure, form and style. How meaning is interpreted and communicated through performance conventions.	What is the play structure? Which style can each scene be performed in?
6	How the text is constructed and how performances create meaning through the characteristics of the performance text, including character, language and dialogue.	Who are the main characters?
7	How meaning is interpreted and communicated through the actor's vocal and physical interpretation of character.	How does an actor prepare for a performance?
8	How the text is constructed and how performances create meaning through the characteristics of the performance text, including character, language and dialogue. How meaning is interpreted and communicated through performance conventions and the actor's vocal and physical interpretation of character.	Who are the other characters? How does an actor multirole successfully?
9	How the text is constructed and how performances create meaning through the characteristics of the performance text, including character, language and dialogue. How meaning is interpreted and communicated through the design of costume and make-up.	Creating costumes for characters.

10	How meaning is interpreted and communicated through the use of performance space and spatial relationships on stage, including the impact of different stages on at least one scene. How meaning is interpreted and communicated through relationships between performer and audience.	Which type of staging would be suitable for a performance?
11	How the text is constructed and how performances create meaning through the characteristics of the performance text, including stage directions. How meaning is interpreted and communicated through relationships between performer and audience.	What are the requirements of staging a performance?
12	How meaning is interpreted and communicated through the design of set (including props)	What set is required for a performance?
13	How meaning is interpreted and communicated through the design of lighting and sound.	What are the lighting and sound requirements for a performance?
14	How meaning is interpreted and communicated through design. The social, historical and cultural context including the theatrical conventions of the period in which the performance text was created.	What is my design concept for a performance?
15	How the text is constructed and how performances create meaning. How meaning is interpreted and communicated.	Performing the opening and close of the play.
16	How the text is constructed and how performances create meaning. How meaning is interpreted and communicated.	Directing and performing a key scene.

Home learning activities

Pre-lesson activities

Lesson	Task
4	'What is youth theatre?' research task.
12	Collect a range of furniture pictures from magazines, catalogues or printed from online.
15	What is the story of the Billy Goats Gruff? What is the message in the story? How does it relate to *Hard To Swallow*?

Post-lesson activities

Lesson	Task
6	Create a Facebook page for Catherine, Anna (or Simon), Maureen or John
10	Draw a diagram of each staging type. Write the advantages and disadvantages under each stage diagram.

Teacher notes

Teacher notes

Hard To Swallow – Lesson 1	
Teacher:	**Date:**
Teaching Group:	**Lesson period:**

Assessment focus: Interpreting Theatre. Component 3 – Section A

Specification content:

How the text is constructed and how performances create meaning through the characteristics of the performance text, including genre.

How meaning is interpreted and communicated through performance conventions.

Lesson Objectives

Students will be able to:

- define documentary theatre
- describe the process of creating a documentary/verbatim play
- create a scene based on a conversation transcript.

Key Words / Phrases

Documentary theatre

Transcript

Lesson Structure

Starter Activity:	10 mins
Group discussion – What is documentary theatre?	
Provide a definition of documentary theatre to students. Do they know any examples of documentary plays, literature or media?	
What topics could make an engaging documentary play?	

Main Lesson:	10 mins
In pairs, students tell their partner what they did from when they got up and when the left for school. The partner writes down what they say (or takes notes). This is a transcript. Together, turn the narrative into a short script of no more than 1 side handwritten. They should include other people that they spoke to that morning. Some of the narrative may be stage directions	

Choose an emotion to convey in the scene. For example, this could be anger, frustration, sadness, happiness, excitement etc. Rehearse the transcript of their morning as a scene with their partner, refining the script as they perform.	10 mins
Show scenes to the class or another group. Ask the audience to name the chosen emotion with a reason why based on the performance.	10 mins
Plenary: What is the process of creating documentary theatre? Discuss as a class or feedback using mini-whiteboards.	5 mins
Other notes:	

Hard To Swallow – **Lesson 2**	
Teacher: **Date:**	
Teaching Group: **Lesson period:**	
Assessment focus: Interpreting Theatre. Component 3 – Section A	
Specification content: How the text is constructed.	

Lesson Objectives
Students will be able to:
 	
   • describe the narrative of sections 1 – 7 of *Hard To Swallow*
   • summarise the key events of the first half of the play.	

Key Words / Phrases Section Narrative	
Lesson Structure	

Starter Activity: Look at the front cover of the script. What could the play be about? Discuss the title and image as a class and agree what the topic of the play is.	5 mins
Main Lesson: Read sections 1 – 7. This can be in groups, or as a class. At the end of each section write one or two sentences to summarise the events in the scene.	35 mins
Plenary: Make a prediction on what will happen in the second half of the play. Share predictions with the class.	5 mins

101

Other notes:

Hard To Swallow – Lesson 3		
Teacher:	**Date:**	
Teaching Group:	**Lesson period:**	
Assessment focus: Interpreting Theatre. Component 3 – Section A		

Specification content:

How the text is constructed.

Lesson Objectives

Students will be able to:

- describe the narrative of sections 8-14 of *Hard To Swallow*
- summarise the key events of the first half of the play.

Key Words / Phrases

Section

Narrative

Lesson Structure

Starter Activity:	
Recap the events in sections 1 – 7.	5 mins
Main Lesson:	
Read sections 8 – 14.	30 mins
This can be in groups, or as a class.	
At the end of each section write one or two sentences to summarise the events in the scene.	
Plenary:	
Create a series of freeze frames (between 3 and 5) which show the main events in the story.	10 mins

Other notes:

Set lesson 4 pre-lesson home learning task.

Hard To Swallow – Lesson 4		
Teacher:	Date:	
Teaching Group:	Lesson period:	
Assessment focus: Interpreting Theatre. Component 3 – Section A		

Specification content:

The social, historical and cultural context including the theatrical conventions of the period in which the performance text was created.

Lesson Objectives

Students will be able to:

- explain the context of youth theatre
- give facts about the playwright of *Hard To Swallow*
- describe the disorder anorexia nervosa.

Key Words / Phrases

Playwright

Youth Theatre

Anorexia Nervosa

Eating Disorder

Lesson Structure

Starter Activity:	
Review pre-lesson task – What is youth theatre?	5 mins

Main Lesson:	
Put a picture of Mark Wheeller on the board. In pairs or threes, list 5 words to describe the man in the picture.	10 mins
Get students to visit Mark Wheeller's website. Were any of their initial descriptions correct?	
Ask students to allocate lines from the About Me section of Mark Wheeller's website. Create a mini documentary style performance of this text. http://www.newwheellerplays.co.uk/Wheellerplays/About_Me.html	5 mins

Create a leaflet for teenagers about anorexia.	20 mins
The following headings can be given as guidance.	
What is anorexia?	
What are the symptoms?	
What treatments are available?	
The following websites are recommended.	
http://www.nhs.uk/conditions/Anorexia-nervosa/Pages/Introduction.aspx	
https://www.b-eat.co.uk/about-eating-disorders/types-of-eating-disorder/anorexia	
https://www.helpguide.org/articles/eating-disorders/anorexia-nervosa.htm	
Plenary:	
Each student to give one fact about anorexia they have learnt today.	5 mins

Other notes:

This lesson can be completed as home learning.

The following sections of this book are linked to this lesson's teaching context:

Chapter 1: Pages 3 – 6, Chapter 2: Pages 13 – 16, Chapter 3: Pages 25 – 32

Hard To Swallow – Lesson 5		
Teacher:	**Date:**	
Teaching Group:	**Lesson period:**	
Assessment focus: Interpreting Theatre. Component 3 – Section A		
Specification content: How the text is constructed and how performances create meaning through the characteristics of the performance text, including structure, form and style. How meaning is interpreted and communicated through performance conventions.		
Lesson Objectives Students will be able to: • describe a range of performance styles • demonstrate their understanding of a performance style • perform a scene in a given style.		
Key Words / Phrases Naturalistic Stylised Physical Theatre		
Lesson Structure		
Starter Activity: Matching activity – Performance styles Ask students to match the performance style with its definition.	5 mins	
Main Lesson: Split students into small groups. Assign a scene to each group. The group reads the scene together and assigns parts. Rehearse the scene in the given performance style. Section 6* – stylised – group of 4 – 6 students. Section 7 – physical theatre – group of 3 students. Section 9 – naturalistic – group of 3 – 5 students. * This is a longer section so the group may be given part of the scene to rehearse and perform.	20 mins	

Perform the scenes to the class.	10 – 15 mins
Plenary: Group discussion – what impact did the scenes have in their chosen performance style?	5 – 10 mins
Other notes:	

Hard To Swallow – **Lesson 6**	
Teacher: Date:	
Teaching Group: Lesson period:	
Assessment focus: Interpreting Theatre. Component 3 – Section A	

Specification content:

How the text is constructed and how performances create meaning through the characteristics of the performance text, including character, language and dialogue.

Lesson Objectives

Students will be able to:

- identify the main characters in *Hard To Swallow*
- describe the main characters and their characterisation
- use examples from the text to support their interpretation.

Key Words / Phrases

Characterisation

Role-on-the-wall

Dialogue

Lesson Structure

Starter Activity: Split the class into 3. Create a role-on-the-wall for Catherine, Maureen and John. Include a minimum of 3 quotes from the text. This activity can be completed in small groups in a larger class. Anna and Simon can also be included in larger classes.	10 mins
Main Lesson: Discuss characterisation of Catherine, Maureen and John. Feedback the role-on-the-wall to the class.	5 mins
In groups of groups of four, create a scene where Catherine, Anna (or Simon), Maureen and John are being interviewed by a reporter for a local TV programme on eating disorders. Include phrases from the play in the characters responses	15 mins

Plenary:	
Perform to the class. Ask the audience to give examples of characterisation from each scene which successfully portrayed the characterisation to the audience.	15 mins

Other notes:

Set home learning task.

Create a Facebook profile page for Catherine, Anna (or Simon), Maureen or John.

Hard To Swallow – **Lesson 7**		
Teacher: **Date:**		
Teaching Group: **Lesson period:**		
Assessment focus: Interpreting Theatre. Component 3 – Section A		

Specification content:

How meaning is interpreted and communicated through the actor's vocal and physical interpretation of character.

Lesson Objectives

Students will be able to:

- describe a range of rehearsal techniques
- demonstrate a given rehearsal technique
- explain how the exercise prepares an actor for a performance.

Key Words / Phrases

Rehearsal Technique

Research

Improvisation

Lesson Structure

Lesson Structure	Time
Starter Activity: Watch Section 10 from the performance. Discusion – What could Maureen be feeling in this scene?	5 mins
Main Lesson: Group discussion – rehearsal techniques. What is the purpose of a rehearsal technique? What does it do to support the performance?	5 mins
In pairs, explore the character of Maureen in Section 10	15 mins
Share the work on rehearsal techniques and discuss what this has told the actor about the character of Maureen.	10 mins

Plenary:	
Make a list of 5 rehearsal techniques from today's lesson and write a description of each one.	10 mins

Other notes:

This blog post contains a comprehensive list of rehearsal techniques suitable for GCSE.
https://roysdrama.blogspot.co.uk/2013/09/rehearsal-techniques.html

A number of techniques are linked to practitioner study, so students may wish to use a technique they are familiar with and have studied before.

Teacher:	**Date:**

Teaching Group:	**Lesson period:**

Assessment focus: Interpreting Theatre. Component 3 – Section A

Specification content:

How the text is constructed and how performances create meaning through the characteristics of the performance text, including character, language and dialogue.

How meaning is interpreted and communicated through performance conventions and the actor's vocal and physical interpretation of character.

Lesson Objectives

Students will be able to:

- describe the features of multirole
- demonstrate multirole in a performance
- explain how to perform multirole successfully.

Key Words / Phrases

Multirole

Lesson Structure

Starter Activity:	
Start standing in a circle. Each students mimes an action which demonstrates a profession. For example, air hostess, driver, teacher, tv presenter.	10 mins
Discuss the use of stereotypes to convey a character to an audience. What else can be used to convey character to an audience?	

Main Lesson:	
Read Section 8: The Brussels Sprout Scene	5 mins
In pairs, act out the scene with one actor as Maureen and the other multirolling the other characters.	15 mins
Spotlight performances and feedback on the use of multirolling.	10 mins

Plenary:	
Group discussion - What makes a successful multirolled performance?	5 mins

Other notes:

Hard To Swallow – **Lesson 9**	

Teacher:	**Date:**

Teaching Group:	**Lesson period:**

Assessment focus: Interpreting Theatre. Component 3 – Section A

Specification content:

How the text is constructed and how performances create meaning through the characteristics of the performance text, including character, language and dialogue.

How meaning is interpreted and communicated through the design of costume and make-up.

Lesson Objectives

Students will be able to:

- describe how meaning can be communicated through costume design
- create a costume for a main character in *Hard To Swallow*.

Key Words / Phrases

Characterisation

Representation

Lesson Structure

Starter Activity: Show students a range of people in costumes. What type of people are they?	10 mins

Main Lesson: Group discussion – how can meaning be communicated through costume design?	5 mins

Choose a character from *Hard To Swallow*. Students will need to decide whether the actor is multirolling or not as this will impact on their design. Design a costume for the character or characters (if multirolling).	20 mins

Plenary: Present costume designs to the class explaining the meaning it is designed to communicate.	10 mins

Other notes:

116

Teacher:	**Date:**

Teaching Group:	**Lesson period:**

Assessment focus: Interpreting Theatre. Component 3 – Section A

Specification content:

How meaning is interpreted and communicated through the use of performance space and spatial relationships on stage, including the impact of different stages on at least one scene.

How meaning is interpreted and communicated through relationships between performer and audience.

Lesson Objectives

Students will be able to:

- describe the features of a range of performance spaces
- perform in a given performance space
- explain the advantages and disadvantages of a range of performance spaces.

Key Words / Phrases

Proscenium Arch

Theatre in the Round

Traverse

Thrust

Promenade

Lesson Structure

Starter Activity: Students arrange themselves as an audience for each of the following stage types: Proscenium Arch, Theatre in the Round, Traverse, Thrust, Promenade. After each stage type, review with students and correct any errors.	10 mins
Main Lesson: Read Section 3: Refusing to Eat.	5 mins
In groups of 3, rehearse a performance of Section 3 (or part of the scene). Each group should be given a different type of staging.	10 mins

117

Perform the scenes to the class. The group should arrange the class before their performance to match the type of staging they have been given.	10 mins
Plenary: Group discussion – what are the advantages and disadvantages of each type of staging.	10 mins

Other notes:

Set home learning task.

Draw a diagram of each staging type. Write the advantages and disadvantages under each stage diagram.

Hard To Swallow – Lesson 11

Teacher:	Date:
Teaching Group:	Lesson period:

Assessment focus: Interpreting Theatre. Component 3 – Section A

Specification content:

How the text is constructed and how performances create meaning through the characteristics of the performance text, including stage directions.

How meaning is interpreted and communicated through relationships between performer and audience.

Lesson Objectives

Students will be able to:

- describe the requirements of staging based on the stage directions
- identify staging requirements from a script
- explain how stage directions can be interpreted by a director.

Key Words / Phrases

Stage Directions

Lesson Structure

Starter Activity: Group discussion - What are stage directions? What are they used for? Why do playwrights include stage directions?	5 mins
Main Lesson: Read a section of the text in groups. Rehearse the scene (or part of the scene) ignoring or contradicting all the stage directions. Section 2 – group of 2 – 6 students. Section 5 – group of 3 – 4 students. Section 11 – group of 3 – 5 students.	10 mins
Feedback discussion – How did the actors perform not using the stage directions? Most groups will have added in their own interpretations as a director would.	5 mins

119

Rehearse the section again following all the stage directions.	10 mins
Spotlight performances.	10 mins
Plenary: Discussion – how did the stage directions impact on the performances?	5 mins
Other notes: Set lesson 12 pre-lesson home learning task.	

Hard To Swallow – Lesson 12		
Teacher:	**Date:**	
Teaching Group:	**Lesson period:**	
Assessment focus: Interpreting Theatre. Component 3 – Section A		
Specification content: How meaning is interpreted and communicated through the design of set (including props)		
Lesson Objectives Students will be able to: • design a suitable set for a performance of *Hard To Swallow* • explain how meaning can be communicated through set design.		
Key Words / Phrases Set Design Properties (Props) Model Box Composite Set		
Lesson Structure		
Starter Activity: In groups, read Sections 1, 12 and 14. Make a list of all the set and prop requirements of the scene. The scenes can be allocated to different groups or each group can look at a combination of scenes.	5 mins	
Main Lesson: Feedback the set lists to the class. Split the list into 'essential' and 'additional' lists.	5 mins	
Different performance styles require different amounts of set design. Group discussion – What is a naturalistic set? What is a non-naturalistic set? What is a composite set?	5 mins	

Split the class into groups of 3 or 4. Ask each group to design a set for a performance.

Draw a ground plan of the classroom space and add in the set design for their performance. | 10 mins |
| Review pre-lesson learning task – collect a range of furniture pictures from magazines, catalogues or printed from online.

How does set communicate meaning to an audience

Create a mood board of set ideas which would be suitable for section 12, the Billy Goats scenes or suitable for the whole play. | 15 mins |
| **Plenary:**

Evaluate the mood boards, stating what the audience may interpret from the designers choices. | 5 mins |
| **Other notes:** | |

Hard To Swallow – Lesson 13		
Teacher:	**Date:**	
Teaching Group:	**Lesson period:**	
Assessment focus: Interpreting Theatre. Component 3 – Section A		
Specification content: How meaning is interpreted and communicated through the design of lighting and sound.		
Lesson Objectives Students will be able to: • describe the lighting and sound requirements for a performance of *Hard To Swallow* • explain how lighting and sound communicates meaning in a performance • create a lighting and sound design for a performance of *Hard To Swallow*.		
Key Words / Phrases Lighting Sound FX Cue Sheet		
Lesson Structure		
Starter Activity: Discussion – What is a cue sheet? Review examples of cue sheets and make a list of its characteristics.	5 mins	
Main Lesson: In groups, create a soundscape for one of the following scenes: A park in the summer, a windy day, a long drive. What sounds were created to show the place given? Explain the difference between diagetic and non-diagetic sounds.	10 mins	
Explain colour theory and the use of lighting to represent emotions. Ask students to match emotions to each colour.	5 mins	

Split the class into 4 groups. Assign a scene and role to each group as follows: Section 4 lighting, Section 4 sound, Section 13 lighting, Section 14, sound. Create a cue sheet for their scene for lighting or sound design.	15 mins
Plenary: Present their designs to the class, explaining why they have used those lighting or sound designs included.	10 mins
Other notes:	

Hard To Swallow – Lesson 14	
Teacher:	**Date:**
Teaching Group:	**Lesson period:**

Assessment focus: Interpreting Theatre. Component 3 – Section A

Specification content:

How meaning is interpreted and communicated through design.

The social, historical and cultural context including the theatrical conventions of the period in which the performance text was created.

Lesson Objectives

Students will be able to:

- describe their design concept for a performance to a modern audience
- explain how their design concept communicates meaning to an audience.

Key Words / Phrases

Design concept

Lesson Structure

Starter Activity:	
What is my vision for the performance?	5 mins
Discuss in pairs or small groups the design elements created from previous lessons	

Main Lesson:	
In fours, work together to decide on the design elements for a performance of *Hard To Swallow*.	30 mins
The following should be considered by the groups:	
Lighting: What feel should the general cover lighting have and does this remain constant? What special lighting effects are required?	
Sound: Will the sound effects be recorded or live? Will the sound reflect the period of the script or will it be modernised?	
Set: Will one set be used or will there be set changes? What will the set look like?	
Costume: Will each character have one costume or will there be costume changes? What will the main characters costumes look like?	
NB. Students should consider a base costume which can be adapted for different characters.	
Plenary:	
Present your design concept to another group or the class	10 mins
Other notes:	
Set lesson 15 pre-lesson home learning task.	

Teacher:	**Date:**

Teaching Group:	**Lesson period:**

Assessment focus: Interpreting Theatre. Component 3 – Section A

Specification content:

How the text is constructed and how performances create meaning.

How meaning is interpreted and communicated.

Lesson Objectives

Students will be able to:

- describe the narrative of the opening and closing scenes of the play
- perform the opening and closing scenes of the play
- explain the subtext of the opening and closing scenes of the play.

Key Words / Phrases

Subtext

Allegory

Foreshadowing

Lesson Structure

Starter Activity:
 	
Review pre-lesson home learning task.
 	
    • What is the story of the Billy Goats Gruff?
    • What is the message in the story?
    • How does it relate to *Hard To Swallow*?
	5 mins

Main Lesson: Group discussion What is subtext? What is allegory? What is foreshadowing?	5 mins
Devise a 'billy goats's scene which could appear elsewhere in the play. This should either reflect on the events up to the scene, or foreshadow the events after it.	20 mins

Plenary:	
Perform the scenes to the class. Ask the audience to feedback on what they have learnt from these scenes.	15 mins

Other notes:

Hard To Swallow – Lesson 16		
Teacher:	**Date:**	
Teaching Group:	**Lesson period:**	
Assessment focus: Interpreting Theatre. Component 3 – Section A		
Specification content: How the text is constructed and how performances create meaning. How meaning is interpreted and communicated.		
Lesson Objectives Students will be able to: • collaborate to direct a performance of a section of *Hard To Swallow* • demonstrate their understanding of how performances create meaning.		
Key Words / Phrases Director Actor Direction Collaboration		
Lesson Structure		
Starter Activity: Divide the class into groups and allocate a different section of the play to each group. Ask the students to assign parts and read through their section.		5 mins
Main Lesson: Rehearse the scene for a performance to the class. Each group should direct themselves. They may decide to nominate a director or two in the group, or may work collaboratively together.		25 mins
Plenary: Perform the scenes to the class. Feedback on the characterisation and how the meaning of the scene was communicated to the audience.		15 mins

Other notes:

Students can be given longer sections, and this task can be completed over a number of lessons.

Epilogue

Loss – Two Mothers from Croydon

By Fiona Spargo-Mabbs mother of Dan, who is the subject of Mark's 2016 play 'I Love You, Mum - I Promise I Won't Die'.

I will never forget meeting Maureen Dunbar on 17 February 2016. There are, sadly, many parents I've met since our son Dan died two years before this, with whom I share the absolute awfulness of having had to bury a precious child. There are many others who have taken this awfulness and made it work for good, in many different ways, in order to try to prevent the same harm happening to others as had happened to their own child, as we have through the drug education charity we set up in Dan's name. There are very few parents in the wide world over, though, who have taken the very strange path of having the story that tells of this awfulness transformed into theatre by Mark Wheeller. And it turns out that two of us live just a few miles apart in Croydon.

I hadn't heard of Maureen, or of the play Mark had written about the death of her daughter Catherine, until he asked if we could include her on our guest list for the premiere of the play he had written about the death of our own son Dan. But then I hadn't heard of Mark Wheeller until Dan's drama teacher suggested the idea for this play. Just as with Catherine's play, Dan's play had been many long months in the making, an incredible, creative and organic process undertaken with such care, commitment and passion by Mark and the talented young people and team of OYT (now not Oaklands but Oasis Youth Theatre) down in Southampton. It was to be premiered at the BRIT School, just a mile or so from our home in Croydon, at the end of March 2016, before an audience of many varieties of importance. Maureen became for me one of the people I most wanted to be there.

Sadly Maureen was unable on the day to come to see our play, but happily we'd met six weeks earlier at her flat nearby. I remember walking through the front door past what seemed like a wall of photographs, some black and white, some colour, Maureen pointing out the beautiful girl that was Catherine. We drank tea, ate biscuits and talked about our lost children, and the journeys on which that loss had taken us. These stories are different in detail, but there was so much that we shared, and the loss of a child at any age and for any reason creates an awful common ground nobody wishes for.

We both spoke mostly about our children. Maureen told me about Catherine's kindness and gentleness and the great strength of her faith, and how her big heart to help others, and her mindfulness of their needs, had remained right up to the very end when she was so weak herself. I wished I could have known her. I did – and do – know the profound strength of Maureen's love for her daughter which spoke, because it's what I know for my son, and which for us both goes on and on forever and is ever-present even though they are both now so very absent. Maureen talked about the very long struggle Catherine had had with anorexia, and how agonising that had been for them all as a family, and especially for her. As a mum who has also lost a precious child I know how totally overwhelming and visceral the longing is to have been able to do absolutely anything in the world to hold onto them and keep them safe.

I told Maureen about my son and his story. Dan had died on Monday 20 January 2014. He was sixteen. He was funny and clever and kind and generous and outrageous and chatty and popular and very, very much loved. A great big dynamic full-of-life presence in our world. On Friday 17 January he had asked to go to a party, but instead he went to an illegal rave the other side of London with a bunch of boys from Croydon. Some of these took MDMA (ecstasy) on the way there. One of these was Dan. What none of them could have known was that the amount of MDMA in the little bag Dan had was lethally strong. He collapsed, was rushed to intensive care, and died two days later from multiple organ failure. We were left with no Dan, a whole heap of questions, and a sense of desperate need to warn other parents about the risks out there for their children, to warn other young people about the risks to them of taking drugs.

Maureen and I also spoke about our plays, which had almost thirty years between them. Maureen told me how she had written and written after Catherine had died. I think her son had bought her a notebook and pen with an instinct this would be something she would need to do. She told me about the unexpected sequence of events that led to these writings becoming published. She told me about how little understanding of eating disorders there was at the time, and how she had wanted to raise awareness of the complexity and desperateness of this condition in the hope this might prevent such a tragedy happening to other families. She'd had the opportunity to work with one of the leading consultants working in this new field. Her openness and honesty and intimate involvement in her daughter's struggle helped him to understand better. Her story has helped many others.

Like Maureen, our play was also borne out of a longing to make this loss make a difference for others. The story of our play really begins with the reporters that knocked on our door first thing the morning after Dan died, and who didn't stop knocking, and our decision to speak to them, to put out this warning message. One of these reporters asked what Dan's last words to me had been, and I knew exactly what they were, because they were what they always were when he went out. Our little jokey exchange. I'd reminded Dan of these over and over in the hospital, of his promise to me. These words then became the headline of the Daily Mail the next day, and were reported in every national paper. They were also to become the title of the play that wasn't yet thought of.

Maureen and I also spoke about the process of the creating of the play. This was different in many ways for us both. Mark had approached her, interested in writing a play about anorexia, and used her book as the primary source. We had approached Mark, with no idea at all how this would all work. On 27 May 2014, what should have been Dan's 17th birthday, his drama teacher, Izzy Forrester, suggested we consider drama as a way of communicating this important message to young people. Dan loved drama, was really good at it, and Izzy was one of the first trustees of our charity. There was a playwright who she said wrote powerfully for young people about issues that affect them, who she'd taught to students for many years, who in fact Dan had studied in drama lessons at school. He was called Mark Wheeller, not a name we knew. We trusted Izzy though, she contacted him on our behalf, and he responded immediately and very positively. We had no idea at that stage though what, if anything, might come of it all, but it felt like the right thing to do.

Trust is enormously important in what is a strange and, at many times, terrifying process. Trust was something else Maureen and I spoke about, and the fierce protectiveness we shared of our children, both of whose stories could easily lead to them being misunderstood, and wrongly judged, in ways that would be heart-breaking but which we wouldn't be able to control. Maureen had the edge on me on calmness and collectedness by many miles, through many more years of knowing Catherine was safe within her story and the play. For me it still felt very fragile and new, and often like handing my son over for public consumption. I needed to know there were safe hands receiving him; that would send him out safely in turn. Being able to trust Mark with our precious stories of our precious children was so important, but something else we both very much shared. It wouldn't have worked without this trust.

I'm sure Maureen and I would also have spoken about the experience of watching the plays that tell the story of the loss of our children, but I'm afraid I can't now remember what Maureen said. I'm sure she was, again, much more composed and calm than I was then, just a few weeks before the first public performances, and the first time for us seeing the play performed in full. For me, watching the play has been so very strange, hard and painful, for all sorts of reasons. This is why I'm very unwilling to see it again. One of the hardest things is seeing someone being me holding

Dan – even if it's an empty hoody. Having him to hold in front of me and it not being real. Hardest of all though is not to be able to get inside the story and change the ending. This Maureen Dunbar also knows, as few others do.

Sadly, the issues of eating disorders are just as relevant thirty years after Catherine's death, and I fear the issues of the risks young people take with drugs and alcohol will still be relevant thirty years after Dan's death. But both Maureen and I have an incredible piece of theatre that communicates these issues powerfully to young people, and which we hope and pray will enable them to keep themselves alive and well. Thanks to Mark Wheeller and to OYT.

More information about the Daniel Spargo Mabbs Foundation at
http://www.dsmfoundation.org.uk

More information about the StopWatch Theatre touring production of I Love You Mum at
https://www.iloveyoumumplay.co.uk

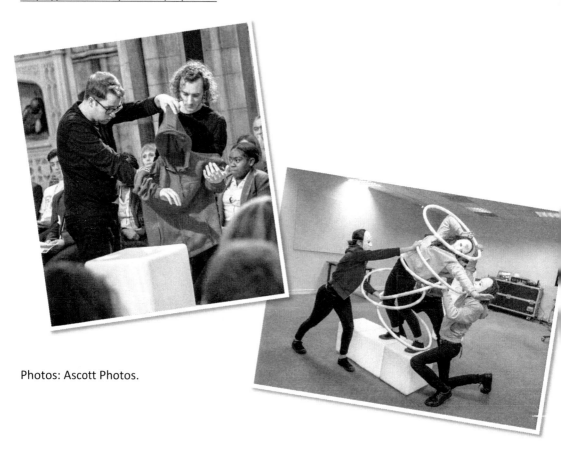

Photos: Ascott Photos.

Appendix 1

Food as a Weapon

Since I was involved in developing *Hard to Swallow*, I have had three children and one grandchild. There have been times when I have found myself in food related battles as the parent. I behaved much as John did in the original situation with Catherine. I had always related closely to his perspective and was very keen to give him a platform at a key point in the play to offer his 'defence'. He had not had this opportunity in the main body of the play. Perhaps it's the fact I'm a male... I'm not sure. This appendix was only included as a result of something unsolicited Sarah sent to me after I'd finished the book. I felt it was worth including.

It would be disingenuous to pretend that food hadn't been used as a bargaining tool in my own house as a young child. If I'd been told off I would storm off in a sulk to my bedroom and refuse to come down to the dinner table. My mother had the "she won't starve, she'll come down when she's hungry" attitude, but my father was noticeably more worried by the idea of my missing a meal. He was a post war baby where food was still scarce and rationed and his way of demonstrating caring for anyone was to cook them a dinner!

Dad would come up to my bedroom and try to negotiate with me to come down and eat. I was aware of the power I gained by holding out and refusing. I don't think anyone knew that in order to keep me going during these stand offs I had a secret collection of sweets in a tin under my bed. E numbers in a wrapper and no substitute for real food, but the artificial flavours took the edge of the hunger just enough for me to be able to torture my parents for longer periods of time when the need arose.

My father became increasingly observant about my eating habits whilst I was playing Catherine. As a youngster, my appetite was always affected by the state of my nerves. The more excited I was, or the more nervous I was (performance days) the less I could focus on eating. I do not come from a family where we discussed anything on an emotional level but I do remember my father getting quite worked up one afternoon when I told him I wouldn't be eating the evening meal with him and his stammering out "You're playing an anorexic, but you're, taking it, you're taking it too far!" ...

> ... *You see, his ears had been pricked by our script. He'd heard, "I'm not hungry, I'll eat later, I've already eaten", too many times inside the theatre!*
>
> *I found this hard to navigate and remember thinking this had been ongoing for John and Catherine for years... and, if it came to it, what could my father do? Physically stuff food into my mouth?*
>
> *How can anyone live in such a sustained sense of daily turmoil? The push and the pull? There's just no middle ground with anorexia, the anorexic is steadfastly dug into one trench at the end of the field and their family members are dug into another, with no-mans land in between.*

Sarah Blackman (Catherine 1989-90)

This made me decide to include my thoughts about the possible impact of doing this play on potential cast members. I have always been concerned that any subject I choose to make a play about COULD have the effect of suggesting or even encouraging the very route that is being flagged up.

In Too Much Punch For Judy, I remember being aware of the possibility that one of the professional cast (who, unlike most of my ETY cast, were drivers) could become involved in a drink-driving incident, never imagining that Judy (the real person dramatised in the play) herself would repeat the same offence on the same stretch of road!!! If speaking out about her accident failed to prevent "Judy" from doing this again, how could I expect anyone merely watching the play to be more affected?

That said, unless they were found to be a general reaction, I would hate to think that any of these might silence such potential for education. I am though working on a hunch (based on how I react to such things) rather than any hard evidence from a detailed study. The whole premise of my personal and professional life is that discussing difficult situations openly is the best way forward. A fear of discussing such issues might silencing them completely! I believe this would be a retrograde step.

Today, just a week before the book goes off to print, this arrived, unsolicited, in response to some publicity for the book. It not only serves as a useful contribution to this chapter but will provide an appropriately positive end... showing that in at least this one case the play HAS been useful.

I started at Hill College (now Taunton's) in September of 1988 and was part of the same A Level Theatre Studies group as Fuzz and Kalwant who were promoting 'Hard to Swallow'. I wasn't expecting anything amazing... it was just a youth group in a school. I was wrong on so many levels. It had a profound effect on me and it stayed with me.

I had spent my secondary school in a boarding school after a messy parental divorce and then moved in with my father. He had a new relationship and bought a house with his partner in Southampton. I ended up in a new situation at Hill College. I knew no-one. I grew an aversion to the sound of eating and became anxious over it. I would become anxious, people would eat, I couldn't eat because I was anxious and round it went. So, without planning anything I barely ate and didn't think much about it. I was losing weight but I was doing a lot of walking so didn't give it a second thought.... until I saw the play.

I spent the first part of the play being a little uncomfortable and the second part trying to keep my eyes shut so I didn't have to watch but could still hear. In less than a couple of hours I realised I had a problem. Eating disorders come in many shapes and sizes. I didn't hide food, make myself sick, not eat deliberately; I'd just got into the habit of not eating. I remember seeing sweets being poured out of a carrier bag in a powerful scene in the play and fixating on a Flake and for years I would associate Flakes with anorexia and never touched one.

Afterwards the cast were out and about after with their families - I studied the girl who played Catherine, her white make-up, her out of role smile and pride in what they had achieved. Yet I was stuck in that theatre - 4 rows up, stage right by the steps. I went home that night and remember feeling nauseous and standing in the bathroom with nothing in my stomach to throw up. Then I talked it through with my dad. From there an appointment was arranged at the doctors and I was watched at meal times. I'd sit at the table in the dining room reading a book to stop my mind overthinking the food and slowly eat a meal, mouthful by mouthful. Do not think that I ever put myself in the category of Catherine. I was small fry but to me it was a mountain and one that took a long time to climb and slide down the other side.

I have no lasting effects from my eating disorder, probably because it didn't get to control me. Maybe it would be a different story if I hadn't seen the play and my realisations would have been too late. One thing is for sure. 'Hard to Swallow' stays with me.

Martha (Member of the audience for OYT's Production in January 1989)

In researching for this play I discovered some un-published Billy Goat scenes. There was also an unfinished Billy Goat poem. I have completed it and decided that this should become the end to

137

this book. In it, I attempt to confront these issues and state my perspective. Thank you for reading the book. I hope it has proved useful. ☺

It used to be said (in the war) Careless Talk Costs Lives. The opposite is also true... Careless Silence Costs Lives too!

Careless Silence Costs Lives[13]

The Billy Goat parents woke up one day
To find their Baby had gone astray
They looked to the left, they looked to the right
But their little Baby was no-where in sight

They looked to the green fields and the mountain slope
Mummy ran inside and grabbed her telescope
Then, sliding into focus they saw Baby's silhouette
High on the magical mountain ledge, frightened and upset

Chasing behind, the troll reached out his hand
Baby thought the troll was scary... he didn't understand...
So, Baby veered towards the edge...

What should the Billy Goats have done?

There was no more edge left...

What should they have done?

Not a millimetre...

What could they have done?

Baby peered into the enchanted ocean, inviting and calm
And felt fear melt inside him as the troll stretched out his arm...

Shout at him!
Make him come home?
Talk him down... Make him...

But before they decided, time ran out...
And left mummy and daddy in no doubt...
Baby Goat was...

---

[13] A performance of this (by RSCoYT), and the other unreleased Billy Goat plays that were developed for the original Hard To Swallow can be found on the Hard to Swallow DVD released in 2016 and available from Wheellerplays@gmail.com. The text for all of the Billy Goat plays can be downloaded from www.resources4drama.co.uk "Crossing the Bridge – Unseen Billy Goats Scenes from Hard to Swallow c. 1988"

Baby Goat… over and out.
Silence costs lives.

The troll meanwhile turned and fled
He knew he'd be blamed and again saw red…

Goats, humans, they're really the same
Trolls appear. They're easy to blame
Skill up in building bridges… Bossing crossing bridges to the green fields…
Cross the Bridge… Boss the bridge… Don't ever stop talking… don't ever stop walking…
Ignore the trolls… easier said than won… and you can win…
Cross the bridge… boss the bridge…
Cross**ed** the bridge.

Appendix 2

Where are they now?

OYT contributors 30 years on...

I went on to live and study Performing Arts in London and performed in numerous theatres around the UK on No.1 tours. I have featured in a handful of films. The working title of the memoirs I threaten to write, about the highs and lows of life on the road, is "Dog hairs in the marmalade jar" referencing to the numerous eye opening and peculiarly unique experiences of staying in theatrical 'digs'.

I returned to Southampton twice. Once to run an inclusive summer Youth Theatre and then to rehearse for the first TIE tour of 'Chicken', with the (then) emerging Stopwatch Theatre Company. With the 'perfect face for radio', I had a weekly slot on London's LBC talk radio station, hosted by Sandi Toksvig, Jenny Éclair and James O'Brien.

I lived in Hong Kong for 4 years devising and directing theatre, before spending three years in India. At the time of going to press I have relocated to the UAE and am currently fostering street cats for an animal protection programme and teaching yoga in the desert. I am still waiting for the National Theatre to give me a call to invite me back!

Sarah Blackman

Life after OYT threw me into a spell at college doing drama but this was short lived and I entered the working world. Now at 44, I am an operations manager for a major highway construction company. Looking back I recognise that my OYT journey developed my social confidence and presentation skills. I use these regularly, presenting and briefing to the contract teams. To stand up and speak to an audience with confidence takes nerve. The only difference now is there is no show curtain to hide behind. I look back at school and wonder what it was all about, but when I look back at OYT I can honestly say it gave me some of my best assets and contributed so much to the person I am today.

Richard Brown

Being a member of OYT has to be one of most poignant experiences which has influenced my life, even to the present day. It gave me the confidence and opportunity to enjoy the beauty of performing and I relished the rush of adrenaline I experienced whilst performing on stage. I went on to study, Theatre studies at "A level" and a "BA honours" degree at Middlesex University.

This in turn, led to touring as an actress and tour manager with Stopwatch Theatre Company working in theatre in education. I also enjoyed many moments in front of the camera, being involved in a variety of small TV projects. I then started working for voice over agencies and found a new confidence as an Operations Manager for a computer company, eventually being responsible for 11 countries. I now have 2 children and work in a Junior school. I'm often being asked to help inject enthusiasm into their school productions and year group assemblies, which is a real joy. My passion for the arts is still deep rooted and is now growing as a seed within both of my children.

Donna McInally

My time in youth theatre definitely played a part in my continued interest in theatre. I went on to study it at A-level and then a Communication Studies degree in London. I had a career in video and TV production, where I still loved the feeling of creative camaraderie! This has now evolved into work as a writer and editor of content for lifestyle and retail brands among others. Now I live in Somerset with my partner and four children.

Debra O'Sullivan

I am now a Deputy Headteacher in North Hampshire. I still believe in the power of theatre to educate and the power of education to transform lives.

Chris Vaudin

About Mark Wheeller

I have been writing since my schooldays at Marlwood Comprehensive School, Bristol. My dream was to be the next Ziggy Stardust. No-one shared my belief in "Eed Sud and The Luminous Earwigs" and I realised no one wanted to hear my songs. I did not give up easily and found people to write plays around them and my friends seemed keen to perform in these musicals! I ran out of friends willing to spend their time writing plays for me so, in 1980 took the plunge myself.

Together with my students over nearly forty years, I have been grappling to find ways of presenting stories to their mums and dads (and various festival adjudicators) that will interest, entertain and inform. Many stories we have told are exceptional and people are at last beginning to see that the way we have told them is exceptional too!

I retired from drama teaching in July 2015 (after 36 happy years) to concentrate on my Wheellerplays, RSCoYT, writing plays and delivering Drama/Theatre workshops across the world.

I live in Southampton with my wife Rachael, have three children (Ollie, Charlie and Daisy), a grandson, Bleu and a Labrador, Dusty.

www.wheellerplays.com
@markwheeller (note the double e double L)

About Karen Latto

I taught a range of creative subjects in secondary education for seven years between 2007 and 2014 across Herts, Essex and Suffolk. During my teaching career I taught Drama, Music, Performing Arts, Media and English across Key Stages 3-5.

In 2014 I joined OCR and lead the development of their new GCSE (9-1) Drama and AS/A Level Drama and Theatre qualifications. This involved writing the specifications and sample assessment materials as well as producing resources to support teachers. I have collaborated with stakeholders including Ofqual and the Department for Education on subject issues and have built prominent links with industry practitioners. I have also engaged with the press, representing OCRs view on Drama to the public, including being interviewed for BBC Radio and being quoted in national and regional newspapers.

In April 2017, I became an Independent Education Adviser and CPD trainer, supporting the work of teachers across the country. I run in-house CPD sessions on curriculum and assessment, and consult on a wide range of education projects. I have also become a governor of a local primary school and joined the National Drama Executive Committee.

In October 2017, I started a Masters of Education at Cambridge University in Educational Leadership and School Improvement.

www.karenlatto.com

Other publications by Mark Wheeller:

Plays

Graham: World's Fastest Blind Runner!	Zinc Publishing
Too Much Punch For Judy	Zinc Publishing
Hard To Swallow	Zinc Publishing
Chicken!	Zinc Publishing
Sweet FA	SchoolPlay Productions
Chunnel Of Love	Zig Zag
Legal Weapon & II	Zinc Publishing
Butcher, Butcher Burning Bright (Arson About)	Oxford University Press
The Gate Escape	Zinc Publishing
Missing Dan Nolan	Zinc Publishing
Sequinned Suits and Platform Boots/(We Were) Ziggy's Band	Resources4Drama
Jamie in The Land of Dinnersphere	Zinc Publishing
Kill Jill	Zinc Publishing
Granny and the Wolf	Resources4Drama
Driven to Distraction	Zinc Publishing
One Million to STOP THE TRAFFIK	Zinc Publishing
The Wheeller Deal - 3 Short Plays, Damon and Bazza Lads, Always in a Hurry & Parents!	Resources4Drama
Wheellerplays – The Author's Definitive Collection (A Collection of Wheellerscenes)	Zinc Publishing
Jack!	Resources4Drama
Silas Marner	Resources4Drama
Chequered Flags to Chequered Futures	Zinc Publishing
Scratching the Surface	Pping
I Love You, Mum I Promise I Won't Die	Methuen
Crossing the Bridge - Unseen Billy Goat Scenes from Hard to Swallow c. 1988	Resources4Drama

Musicals

King Arthur - All Shook Up	SchoolPlay Productions
Blackout	SchoolPlay Productions
No Place For A Girl	SchoolPlay Productions
The Most Absurd Xmas Musical In The World... Ever!	SchoolPlay Productions
Wacky Soap	Zinc Publishing/Resources4Drama

Productions on YouTube

Blackout – Operation Pied Piper
Wacky Soap

DVDs

Wheellerplays Exemplified
Graham - Worlds Fastest Blindman!
Wheellerplays – The Definitive Collection
One Million To STOP THE TRAFFIK
Too Much Punch For Judy
Jack (Physical Theatre – no recognisable words)
Chequered Futures to Chequered Flags/Chicken (Double bill)
Bang Out Of Order by Johnny Carrington & Danny Sturrock.
Missing Dan Nolan
I Love You, Mum – I Promise I Won't Die
Scratching the Surface
Hard To Swallow

DVD's of Mark's work now available from Pping Publishing at www.wheellerplays.com or email
<u>Wheellerplays@gmail.com</u>

Books

Tufty's Adventures	RoSPA
Wacky Soap Storybook	Zinc Publishing
Drama Schemes	Rhinegold
The Drama Club	Pping/Resources4Drama
The Story Behind…Too Much Punch For Judy	Pping
Hard to Swallow – Easy to Digest	Pping

Other Titles by Pping Publishing

Scratching the Surface (Pping Publishing)

Scratching the Surface is now available from Mark Wheeller *(wheellerplays@gmail.com)* as a script and as a DVD.

"It is important that everyone feels able to talk about mental health issues - they affect one in four of us - and plays like the excellent, "Scratching the Surface", are really important in giving mental health, particularly in how it affects younger people, the attention it deserves and needs."
Solihull MIND

This new verbatim play by Mark Wheeller dramatises the story of his interviews with Rob, a young man who, as a teenager, self-harmed. Mark chats to his family as they reflect on the trauma of living with this constant "elephant in the room", as they describe it. Mark then went on to talk with a group of randomly selected students from a school in the Midlands. This encounter was equally shocking as gradually all of them admitted they had either encountered someone who had self harmed or had themselves self harmed. One thirteen year old described it as "the mouse in the room"

A Verbatim Play by

Mark Wheeller

Commissioned by Alderbrook School

"You feel like a small helpless being, to the point that you'd hurt yourself and everyone around is different to you."

"Great play that my students have really engaged with. I've never had Year 9 ask to keep reading a play rather than getting up to do practical. They found it fascinating and said they thought it was great the way the play used the teenagers own words. Really recommend to anyone working in a high school."
Amazon Verified buyer review.

The Drama Club (Pping Publishing)

The Drama Club is now available from Mark Wheeller *(wheellerplays@gmail.com)* or Clive Hulme *(www.resources4drama.co.uk)* as a book with plenty of downloads!

This is the record of a project which Mark Wheeller never wanted to be involved in - a Junior School Drama Club - but which resulted in a triumph. Mark takes us through the process of what happened step by step and gives practical advice on running a similar project in your own school or club. The book includes a 10 scene, multi-actor script and access to an online support pack from Resources4Drama. This is an ideal source book for those looking for inspiration to run their own extra-curricular Drama activities with children and young people. The innovative guide guarantees parental involvement and appreciation.

"I must admit that when I first opened the package my heart sank, I was hoping for something a little....bigger. Nevertheless, in the old adage of don't judge a book by its cover (or its size) I gave it a read. I have taught drama for over 20 years and although I love my subject, can often get stuck in a rut. This book gave me a different perspective on how to approach drama with this age range. I was really impressed with some of the new ideas and at their simplicity too. Not only are the ideas there but a 10 scene script that you can start putting into practice immediately. My drama class will be working with and adapting Midnight to suit them this term.... I really am excited about trying out some of the projects in this book and would wholeheartedly recommend. Concluding that size really doesn't matter after all! Well done Mark Wheeller and Clive Hulme on creating a really different drama book worth every penny."
Amazon Verified Reviewer.

147

The Story Behind – Too Much Punch for Judy (Pping publishing)

The Story Behind – Too much Punch for Judy is now available from Mark Wheeller *(wheellerplays@gmail.com)*

Too Much Punch for Judy has become one of, or perhaps even the, most performed contemporary play. It has been performed 6020 times (August 2017) since it was first shown in a 30 seat school drama studio in 1987. Messages from students studying the play asking about its background sparked Mark Wheeller's initial interest to write this book. You will discover the story behind the play is quite a story.

Barrie Sapsford, who was in the original Epping Youth Theatre production, has designed this book to make it attractive and accessible.

"As a GCSE Performing Arts Teacher often it is difficult to find teaching materials that really meet the needs of the students I teach. I have long been a fan of Mark Wheeller and in particular "Too Much Punch For Judy". This book to accompany the play is quite simply a gift. It offers invaluable insight into how the play was created, the creative processes that were undertaken to stage it and most importantly the playwright's journey from page to stage. The course I teach at GCSE is vocational and requires the students to fully understand the demands of working as a professional in this Industry and this book is immensely useful. I highly recommend this to all Drama Teachers!"

Amazon Verified Reviewer

The story of *Too Much Punch for Judy*

*"**May 20th 1983:** A lonely Road near Epping. A Renault 5 comes off the road and hits a bridge. The scaffolding construction slices through the windscreen. The driver, Judy, escapes unhurt but the passenger, her sister Joanna, is killed outright. Jo and Judy had both been drinking.*

***5th October 1993:** Judy is involved in a second drink drive incident, a head on collision on the same stretch of road. Judy was driving on the wrong side of the road and had suffered only minor injuries. The 21-year-old driver of the other car, who was not drunk, was killed instantaneously."*